Escape to Sandy Bay

BOOK 1 IN THE SANDY BAY SERIES

EMILY HUSSEY

WINSOME BOOKS

Copyright © 2023 Emily Hussey

ISBN 978-0-648297246

Cover Design: D Shorne

Images: Depositphotos

Published by Winsome Books 2024

Adelaide, South Australia

CONTENTS

Also by Emily Hussey

The Red Centre Series
Journey to the Heart
The Red Heart
Trust Your Heart
Follow Your Heart

Stand-alone Titles
Ambition and Passion
Maison Angelique

Harrow Series
Wild Spirit
Wild Destiny
Wild Tempest
Wild Fire

Sandy Bay Series
Secrets in Sandy Bay
Escape to Sandy Bay
Return to Sandy Bay

1 – Visit to Sandy Bay

DRIVING TO A popular coastal town on a Saturday was madness. Alyssa knew that, but here she was. The usual weekend visitors crowded the street, clustering outside the fish and chips café and the ice cream shop. She cruised slowly down High Street, looking on either side for the bakery. She couldn't turn up empty-handed. Perhaps an apple crumble? And flowers… she should have brought flowers. Why wasn't she more organised? Life, that's why.

A flash of red on the road caught the corner of her eye and instinctively her foot hit the brake before she'd fully registered what it was. A small boy in a red t-shirt stood in front of the car. He'd begun to dash across the road, but now he stood in front of her bonnet, frozen and wide-eyed. As she breathed out to calm the adrenaline charge, a man leapt from the footpath and grabbed the boy by the arm, dragging him back to safety. He threw an accusing glare over his shoulder.

Alyssa reacted before fully registering her actions. She threw open her car door and with one foot on the road, levered herself upright so she could eyeball the man over the roof of her sedan. Her heartbeat still raced.

"Keep a tighter grip on him in future. He nearly gave me a heart attack, dashing out like that."

"I'm sorry," he called, now safely back on the footpath. "He was distracted… we both were." He still gripped the boy's arm. "It won't happen again."

"Your wife shouldn't let either of you out without a leash."

Not waiting for a reply, she slipped back into the driver's seat, noting the bank up of cars behind her. She threw the car into gear and accelerated away, not looking in their direction again. When she spied the bakery a short distance further down the main street, she pulled into a carpark and sat for a while, massaging a spot in the middle of her forehead. A nagging tension headache threatened to make the rest of the day miserable.

Put on your big girl pants Alyssa. Just get on with it. It hadn't been easy getting away this weekend and the stress of the preceding week still sat heavily on her shoulders. She would be glad when she could sit for a while and simply be. She took a couple of deep breaths, exhaling slowly before climbing out of the car and braving the crowd in the shop.

Ten minutes later, she laid the paper bag containing an apple strudel cake on her passenger seat and put a flower pot of mixed herbs in the footwell. She drove the remaining distance to her godmother's cottage at a sedate pace, with deference to her purchases.

When she drove up the steep driveway leading to the clifftop cottage, Mary burst from the front door, waving from the deck at the top of the wooden stairs. Alyssa grabbed the bag with the crumble and the flower pot and headed up the stairs to where Mary waited. She could come back later for her bag.

"You're here at last! It's been so long."

Her godmother grabbed her in a bear hug, and the two women rocked gently from side to side, absorbing each other's scent and body heat.

"Come inside. I'll put the kettle on. You must be dying for a cuppa after that drive."

Peeling herself away from the embrace, Alyssa gingerly inspected the contents of the paper bag. The crumble now looked squashed and crumblier.

"I brought us some morning tea, but it looks a little crushed after that welcome."

"It will taste just as good, I'm sure. I've made up your room. Dump your things in there and then I'll catch up with your news. I want to hear it all."

After first leaving the pot of herbs on the kitchen counter, Alyssa slipped back down the stairs to grab her overnight bag and left it in the bedroom. She glanced around the room, looking for any changes. The same handmade quilt was on the bed. She'd loved sleeping here as a child. A photo of herself and Mary, taken when she was about twelve, sat on the dressing table. The room held so many memories. Everything was as she remembered.

The morning sun streamed in through the window, and she stood for a while, re-acquainting herself with the view over the coastline. This scene had greeted her every morning of her visits. She could see all the way down to Pt Reilly and beyond, depending on the weather.

Mary had loaded the cups and coffee pot onto a tray by the time she came back out to the living area. The open plan room incorporated the kitchen, dining and living room and faced the sea.

"I thought we might sit out on the deck. There's no wind today."

Mary led the way to the sliding doors carrying the tray. Alyssa followed with the apple crumble and a couple of serving plates. When the day was fine, they took meals out on the deck, and usually did when Alyssa made the trip to Sandy Bay. Not as often as she meant to. Tiger, her godmother's fat tabby feline occupied one of the chairs, soaking up the morning sun. Mary poured the coffee and the two women settled back on their respective chairs.

"I have so missed this outlook," Alyssa said after downing the first gulp of her coffee. "Once I'm seated here, I can feel the pressures of the city start to wash away."

"Pressures of the city… that bad, huh?" Mary sounded concerned.

"I don't mean to make it sound worse that it really is, but you know… there's the traffic, and work politics and never enough time for anything. The world seems to slow down in Sandy Bay."

"And Phillip? You haven't mentioned him."

"He's fine. We both lead busy lives, so it's difficult to connect sometimes, but we're solid."

"Is marriage on the cards still? You mentioned it last year but I haven't heard anything since then."

Alyssa sipped her coffee. How to answer when she didn't really know herself. It wasn't that Phillip was being evasive, but he always seemed too busy or too tired to discuss their plans. "It's not a high priority for us," she said eventually. "We're happy as we are."

"If you're thinking of children, you're leaving it a bit late," her godmother said softly. "I know children aren't for everyone, but I would hate for you to lose the option through some man not being able to commit." She reached for a knife and cut a slice of the strudel. "It's not any of my business, I know, so I won't say any more about that. It's up to you how you live your life."

They settled into an uneasy silence. Out in the bay, a trio of surfers rode the waves, and further out a flotilla of fishing boats were anchored near the reef. Alyssa was relieved that some things never changed, even if there was increased housing development, as she'd noticed on her drive into the town. Possibly an increase in retirees.

"So, what's your news? What's been happening in and around Sandy Bay since I was last here?"

"Not much of note. There's a new gym opened up, and a new ice cream parlour in town. That interests me more than the gym, to be honest. It's what's about to happen that's more of interest."

"What do you mean? What's about to happen?" Alyssa helped herself to some of the strudel. If she had too much, she could always try out the new gym."

Mary gestured with a nod of her head to the headland below them. It was a tract of natural vegetation leading to a cliff overlooking a secluded section of the bay. The locals had worn a path through there, and years ago some of the residents had combined to build a staircase down to the cove below.

"Discussions are underway between council and a local company to develop a coastal resort over that land. It will impede our view and the locals will lose access to the beach."

Alyssa looked from her godmother to the land in front of them and back again to the older woman. "But isn't that Council land? It's not zoned for a development of that nature. How could this happen?"

Mary pulled a face. "Money talks, you know that. Prestige Developments own a parcel of land on the outskirts of town. It's farming land but has potential for residential development, and the Council wanted Prestige to allocate a portion of it for social housing."

She reached out and massaged Tiger's head. "A deal was done. Prestige offered to swap the land they already owned, for this portion in front of us. They're planning an up-market development overlooking the coast. The Councillors found the offer attractive. The farming land is large enough to support a new subdivision. The Council can do a detailed urban plan incorporating parks and reserves, a walking trail and a commercial precinct. There is provision for a school and all sorts of desirable features. The council plans to rezone it for residential use."

"Are you sure it's a done deal?" Alyssa's incredulous tone betrayed her indignation.

"I don't believe so. An option agreement has been signed, but not a contract. It's subject to the state planning department agreeing to the rezoning of our land. If that doesn't happen, the deal's off."

"Our land…" Alyssa repeated. "It is our land. That land belongs to the community. The Council has no right to dispose of it in this manner. It's currently available to everyone, and if that development goes ahead, it will only be available to those rich enough to stay in a resort. What's the community doing about that?"

"There's been a community meeting, but no firm action evolved from that. A few letters were written to the paper. It really needs someone to lead the charge." She looked hopefully at Alyssa. "You'd be able to advise people how to go about it."

Alyssa held up her hands defensively. "Hey, don't look at me. My life is hectic enough as is and something like that is too difficult to work on from the city."

Tiger woke and jumped off his chair. He stretched, first his spine in the pose of the cat, and then each paw stretched out in front of him. That routine completed, he strolled to the sliding door and sat there expectantly. He flicked the end of his tail. *Come on human, open the door for me.*

Alyssa rolled her eyes but obligingly stood up and opened the door for the cat. "Is this what I'm reduced to, being a cat butler?"

"That brings me to something I need to discuss with you," Mary began. "I've been planning a holiday for some time now.

I want to do a cruise around Norway and up into the Arctic Circle. The Northern Lights are on my bucket list and if I don't go soon, I'll be too old and I'll miss my chance."

"You, too old? Never." Alyssa paused uncertainly. "There aren't any health issues you haven't told me about, are there?"

Her godmother leaned over and patted her hand. "Only the usual aches and pains. Nothing to worry about. I've attended a few funerals in the last twelve months, and that tends to sharpen the focus. I've made up my mind. I'm going to experience Christmas at the North Pole while I'm still able."

"Wow! I'm a little envious. That would be a fabulous trip. You'll need to put your will and power of attorney in order before you go. Did you need help with that? Is that what you wanted to discuss with me?"

Mary laughed. "Working where I have been, you don't think I would have neglected to put that paperwork in order before this?"

Until recently, Mary was employed as an office manager with Densley and Associates, a legal firm in the neighbouring town of Pt Reilly. "Robert Densley made sure years ago that I had all that stuff in order. That's not what I wanted to talk about. I need a house and cat sitter while I'm away. I thought I might talk you into spending some time down here. With side tours that I want to take, I should be away from Australia for around three months, perhaps more. Tiger needs someone to look after him for that time, and the garden needs to be watered. I'd be much happier if the house was occupied."

"Mary, I'd love to help you out, but my job is in the city. Living down in Sandy Bay wouldn't be workable." Then there was Phillip to consider. How would he react if she disappeared down the coast for three months? It wasn't feasible.

"I thought about that, and I have a suggestion. You're always talking about the pressures in your current job. Coincidentally, there's a short-term vacancy coming up with Densley and Partners. I was talking to Paul, Robert's son, about my plans and he mentioned that one of the partners is taking time off with maternity leave. He's looking for a replacement. I mentioned you and he's interested in having a chat. I think you know him, anyway."

"That's kind of you, but I can't take any leave of absence from my current job. The legal world is cut-throat. If I took time out from the city like that, I'd be regarded as light-weight and I'd never get back in. It took me so long to be promoted to associate level."

She eyed off another piece of apple strudel before deciding against it. She wouldn't fit her business suits if she didn't watch out. "Paul and I studied at Uni together, so yes I do know him."

"You don't have to decide straight away," Mary said persuasively. "Think it over and give me a call next week. If you've finished your coffee, it's time for a walk. That will blow the city cobwebs away."

Mary was right about that. She'd been coming to Sandy Bay for years, having spent many childhood holidays there. That was with her parents. Since then, she'd come down when time and opportunity were available, and she always returned to the city much refreshed. She and Mary had a great relationship, and that strengthened after her mother died.

Alyssa changed her shoes, and the two women walked along the path across the headland opposite the house. When she was a child, she had secret places in the scrub, meeting up with some of the local children to play in their cubby houses. It was incomprehensible to think that it all might be razed for future development. There must be some way of stopping it.

When they reached the wooden staircase, they descended to the beach, and strolled along the pristine sand that gave the town its name. Alyssa carried her sandals in her hand and running down to the water's edge, let the wavelets wash over her feet. The water frothed and foamed around her ankles with a soft, salty tickling. It would have been nice if Phillip came down for a weekend break as well, but for some unknown reason, he and Mary had never got along. They were polite with each other, but the atmosphere was uncomfortable. It was easier if she and Mary spent time together without him.

They drove down to the neighbouring town of Pt Reilly that evening, and ate at the Commodore Hotel. As pub meals went, they were very good, and dinner there had been a regular ritual whenever she visited. It didn't disappoint this time either and Alyssa risked a glass of Sauvignon Blanc, even though she was driving. These weekend trips always evoked a holiday feel. A pity she couldn't do it more often. Mary outlined her planned trip and they discussed the must-see locations she ought to build into her itinerary.

"It's a wonderful opportunity. You deserve it after all the work you've put in over the years. I've not known you to take a decent holiday before."

"I've never had the time or money before. I can't tell you how much I'm looking forward to this. You will think about my suggestion, won't you? Tiger knows you, and I have a feeling that a break like this would do you good. That city firm strikes me as a soul-destroying place."

Alyssa felt a flash of irritation. She'd said she would think about it, even though she knew already what her answer would be. It would be crazy to leave her job, and requesting leave without pay would be suicidal. Her answer had to be no. She smiled non-committedly and suggested they look at the dessert menu.

She rose early the next morning and headed down to the beach for a swim. The day promised to be warm, but the cold water made her gasp when she braced herself and dived under an incoming wave. Once the initial shock passed, she was able to indulge in a leisurely swim towards the breakwater and back again. By the time she dragged herself out and towelled dry on the sand, she felt invigorated and ready for a leisurely breakfast.

She didn't have the beach to herself. There were a couple of surfers and some people paddled at the water's edge. Dog walkers kept up a pace behind their canine charges, some dogs on leads, and some chasing out smelly bits of seaweed or dead crabs perhaps. A man and child walked behind an enthusiastic Labrador that raced ahead, and then circled back in an endless loop of tongue-lolling energy. It reminded her of the man and boy she'd seen in the main street the day before. They were probably weekend tourists. She grabbed her towel and headed for the stairs.

Alyssa and Mary took their breakfast out on the deck. While Alyssa had been at the beach, Mary had prepared up a pan of scrambled eggs with slices of smoked salmon, accompanied by her home-made bread. She waited until Alyssa had showered before putting the pan on the stove and cooking the eggs to perfection. She decorated the top with sprigs of parsley before bringing the plates to the table. Tiger sat up in his chair, clearly expecting food to be delivered in his direction as well.

By late morning, Alyssa realised the stresses of the week… probably the month… were easing. She knew she should take breaks from the city more often, but fitting in with Phillip's schedule could be difficult. She would talk to him about it when she got home. If they blocked out the time in advance, it would be doable. It didn't have to be at Sandy Bay; there were heaps of options.

About an hour later, her phone rang, interrupting her research into weekend destinations. She swiped the screen, expecting the caller to be Phillip. It wasn't. Her boss's name appeared as caller ID.

"Morning Michael. This is unexpected. Is everything all right?"

"Sorry to disturb you on a Sunday, but I'm working on the Jamieson report. We have to deliver it by tomorrow and there are some recommendations that could be problematic. Can you review them asap and get back to me pronto?"

"I'm not home. I'm down the coast."

"Don't you have your laptop with you?"

"No, I don't. This is a break from work, and incidentally it's my personal time."

He gave a derisive laugh. "There's no such thing as personal time in this job, you know that. It's up to you how you do it, but I need a response by this evening."

Alyssa stared at the phone after disconnecting the call. He was right. The job demanded on-call dedication. If you wanted to get ahead in the legal profession, that work ethic was expected of you, but it could be so exhausting and draining. She had no other choice. She would have to drive back to the city immediately after a quick lunch.

She made regretful apologies to Mary, and packed her bag. The journey home was quicker than the drive down to Sandy Bay, as she avoided the late Sunday weekend traffic. She used the time to mentally review her input to the report and how she might reframe the contentious issues. It galled her to have her work questioned like this. She had given her professional opinion, and that should stand.

She was still mulling over how she would address the task when she pulled into the driveway of the townhouse she shared with Phillip. A strange car was parked outside, but it probably belonged to a visitor from one of the other townhouses on their block. Parking was always in high demand. She let herself in the front door, and looked around for Phillip. There was no sign of him, but a couple of wine glasses sat on the coffee table. That was odd. He hadn't mentioned a visitor in their call the previous evening. He must be upstairs.

"Phillip?"

As she climbed the stairs, she heard a muffled sound and then a voice that she knew to be his.

"Fuck!"

An inexplicable feeling of dread swept over her. The bedroom door was closed, but she knew that whatever lay behind it, she wasn't going to like what she saw. An icy hand of fear gripped her belly as she threw open the door. Phillip and a strange woman lay in a tangle of sheets, staring at her in horror. The woman clutched the sheets over her breasts in a weak attempt at modesty. Phillip just stared.

It was all Alyssa could do not to vomit on the spot. She didn't say anything. What was the point? It was over. As she stumbled down the stairs, Phillip followed her to the landing, leaning over the balustrade. He was naked.

"Alyssa, wait. I can explain. It's not what you think."

"It's exactly what I think. Put some clothes on, Phillip. You look ridiculous."

She picked up her laptop and walked out the door. At least she was already packed.

2 – On the Headland

TIGER HAD BEEN fed and the pot plants watered. Alyssa checked that the back door was locked and all the lights were switched off. Usually, she flew out the door at around seven o'clock, but it was now a quarter past eight, and she'd been procrastinating for the last thirty minutes.

She checked her image in the hallstand mirror, adjusting the collar of her jacket. She looked neat and tidy… professional. *It will be a breeze. No more complicated mergers or take-overs. Welcome to conveyancing, family law and general legal advice. How hard could that be?* Hell, she might even get some commercial agreements to draft. Working life could possibly be exciting in Pt Reilly.

She didn't normally feel apprehensive. Recent events had shaken her self-confidence, to the point where she doubted her abilities in a range of areas. She obviously sucked at relationships. What if colleagues in the city had known of Phillip's infidelity before she did? The thought humiliated her, but no way would she ask anyone. That would expose her as insecure and an emotional wreck. Which she was. *For Chrissake, put on your big girl pants, Alyssa.* She picked up her car keys.

Pt Reilly was a short drive down the coast from the village of Sandy Bay. Fifteen minutes later, she pulled up in the office carpark, conveniently located behind the building. In the city, carparks were allocated on the basis of seniority; here even the receptionist scored a park. That same woman looked up with a welcoming smile as she entered the reception area.

"Good morning—no trouble finding the office in busy downtown Pt Reilly?" She laughed at her own joke. "I'm Jodie. Follow me and I'll show you to your office. Then Paul would like to have a chat. His office is next to yours."

"Thank you. I remember where his office is from my last visit." As she followed Jodie down the hall, a cloud of cheap perfume wafted over her. Alyssa tried not to sneeze, and her nose itched. That was the first thing she would have to change about the office. She hadn't come all this way to wallow in hay fever.

Jodie threw open the door of what was presumably her new office, and stood to one side. Alyssa squeezed past her and surveyed her new domain. A window to the street front replaced the expansive view over one of the city squares that she was used to. The room was stuffy, as though the door had been shut for too long. She scanned the wall and found the switch for the ceiling fan. Circulating air might help. Hopefully, either the kitchen or a local café produced decent coffee. She already felt as though she needed a double shot.

She turned back to Jodie, hovering in the doorway. "I'll get myself settled, thanks."

She wanted some time alone before seeing Paul. Jodie gave a brief nod, and left, not shutting the door behind her. Alyssa withdrew her laptop from its bag and opened it on her desk. She took out her favourite pen and a notebook and put those on the desk also. The office chair needed adjusting, and she fiddled with the control levers until satisfied with the height and angle of the seat and back rest.

Her predecessor's framed certificates hung on the walls, declaring qualifications and professional memberships. Alyssa took them down and blew away the dust that sat on top of the frames. She had never been one to put her credentials on the wall. Her artworks were in storage back in Adelaide but on her next visit she would retrieve a couple of pictures and put them up here instead. That would mark her territory and make the office her own. She would also pick up a couple of potted plants. She needed greenery around her to maintain her sanity.

Paul looked up with a welcoming smile as she rapped lightly on his door. He rose from his seat and strode around to her side of his desk, hand outstretched. "Welcome aboard. I'm pleased you accepted my offer. I know it's different to the pace and case load you're used to, but you'll soon adjust."

"I'm looking forward to it," she replied smoothly. "It's time for a change in a few areas of my life."

A bemused expression flittered across his face before he picked up a bundle of files from his desk and pushed on. "I'll hand these over to you. Read through to familiarise yourself. Any questions, give me a shout. Otherwise, Jodie can tell you where things are kept and who's who around town. Veritable font of information, that woman is."

"I'll keep that in mind. This pile will keep me entertained for a while. All I really want to know now is where's the best coffee in town?"

He laughed. "There are plenty of cafés down the main street, but you don't have to go out. We have an espresso machine in the kitchen. Jodie will show you how to drive it. While we're on the subject of food, Jacinta said she'll drop in tomorrow morning and take you out for morning tea. I think she's intending to give you the lowdown on life on the coast."

"Morning tea! I'm impressed. It doesn't exist in the city. Don't worry; I'll work late to make up for lost time."

She picked up the bundle of files and took them back to her desk. Once she got that coffee sorted, she could work her way through them. She took a deep breath and exhaled slowly. She could do this. Living in Sandy Bay and working in Pt Reilly for a while would be fine. She had always loved her holidays with Mary, and the city was only a ninety-minute drive away. It would be living the dream. "Keep telling yourself that, girl," she muttered to herself, "keep telling yourself."

❧

The week ran better than she expected. The quick commute won hands down over the city version, and by the end of the week, she had sussed out choice routes for a lunchtime walk. She usually packed her lunch at home, but preferred not to eat it at her desk. People made eye contact and nodded greetings in the street as she passed, and that was a welcome change. She had the feeling that a few of them already knew who she was, given how effective the grape vine could be in a small town.

She enjoyed interacting directly with clients, rather than dealing with corporate intermediaries, and began to understand that what she did could really make a difference to some people's lives. Really, it was what the law should be about. Negotiating the sale of a commercial fishing licence was something different, but she had lots of allied experience to fall back on.

Catching up with Jacinta had been constructive. Paul's wife had moved to Pt Reilly a couple of years earlier, and she promised to introduce Alyssa to her book club and to clue her in on the best coffee houses and her recommendations for grocery and other shopping. They had met a couple of times in recent weeks while Alyssa negotiated her position with Densley and Partners, and the two women had clicked. It had given her positive vibes about the move.

It occurred to her that she could even develop some interests in the evenings, rather than coming home late, collapsing with a drink and a brief chat with Phillip and then sliding into bed before getting up and doing it all over again. Maybe she could write that novel she'd always talked about.

On the first Saturday morning, she followed Jacinta's advice, and shopped early at the local farmer's market before the best produce sold out. An enticing smell led her to the bakery stall, where she bought a still-warm sour dough loaf. It was all she could do not to break it open and dig into the loaf with her fingers.

The cheese stall came next, with rounds and wedges of artisan cheeses made from goat, sheep and cow milk. She tasted them all before settling on a round of brie with ash coating. When her shopping basket was full, including with seasonal fruit and vegetables, she headed towards one of the local café's intending to treat herself to eggs benedict and a cup of coffee brewed from locally roasted beans.

She scored a window seat, and in-between browsing the pages of the weekend paper, indulged in people watching. Tourists and locals alike wandered past the window, all seemingly in a relaxed frame of mind. The realisation that the weekend was totally hers meaning she could do whatever she wanted evolved gradually, and she liked it. Perhaps Sandy Bay was a coastal Shangri-La. Traffic began to bank up outside her window, signally the arrival of weekend visitors. It wasn't quite the mythical paradise, but it was close enough for now.

Tiger demanded attention when she returned to the clifftop cottage. Possibly the fish fillets she'd purchased were part of the reason. Alyssa put the shopping away, and turned her attention to the cat.

"Is it me you love, Tiger, or the fish I just brought home? I'll have you know that's my dinner, but if you play your cards right, there might be some fishy treats for you as well."

The cat rubbed against her legs with a deep, rumbling purr. He had the bearing of an animal who knows and understands his status in the world, and that included regular head-rubs as well as the finest fillets of fish on demand. Whatever his expectations, Alyssa opened a tin of tuna for him, and after twitching his tail for a second, the cat consented to eat it.

That taken care of, she decided on a walk along the beach. Exercise would work off some of the indulgent breakfast. She made her way down the driveway and onto the path leading across the headland towards the beach. On either side of the path, hidden from general view were the secret playgrounds from her childhood. Sometimes, she and her friends had picnics there, and one year, they even camped the night in their cubby. That was a real adventure. No children shrieked or chattered in their secret cubbies today. Except for birdlife and the buzz of insects, the area appeared to be deserted.

Sand dusted the stairs leading down the cliff-face to the beach. Alyssa paused at the top, surveying the scene below. A couple of dog-walkers strolled with their pooches, and a lone fisherman stood just beyond the reach of the waves with his rod extending out into the water. The day's crowds hadn't yet arrived.

After descending the stairs to the beach, she slipped off her sandals and trudged through the sand to the water's edge and paddled in the shallows, treating it as a form of mineral bath. On the walk to the jetty and back, she picked up a pretty fan shell and two plastic straws which had been embedded in the sand. She made a mental note to bring a bag on future walks in which to carry any bits of rubbish she picked up.

On impulse, after emerging at the top of the stairs, she decided to bring back a book, a cold drink and a couple of snacks and to sit in one of the old favourite haunts on the clifftop. It overlooked the harbour and was sheltered from general view. She carried down a fold-up chair as well; she wasn't as comfortable sitting on the ground as she had been when a child.

Why did people travel to overseas coastal destinations when they had this view available? No clouds marred the blue sky; it seemed even bluer than it did in the city if that was possible. The air was so clear, and the colours of the sand and water showed up with sharp clarity. Alyssa read for a while, and then found herself drifting off. The warm sun had a soporific effect that was hard to resist. She pulled her hat lower to shield her eyes, slid down in her seat and snoozed. If only this weather would last.

Perhaps he made a noise or maybe her sixth sense alerted her to an intruder. She jerked awake; her muscles tensed as she tried to work out what had disturbed her, or who. She turned her head slowly so as not to attract attention. She couldn't see anything untoward, but could hear a voice, a soft male voice somewhere very close. She managed to raise herself to a standing position without the chair creaking.

Peering over the shrubbery, she saw a man. He appeared to be alone, and talked to himself as he went about his business. Just her luck to encounter a looney when she was alone in the scrub. Next minute, he squatted down out of her line of vision. What on earth was he doing? Surely not. She hesitated unsure whether to stay quiet and hope that he went away, or to gather up her things and head back to Seaclusion Cottage.

He stood again and she noted with relief that his trousers were belted around his waist with no sign they had been removed. She watched him a while longer. He took a series of photographs of the harbour, the water's edge, and the foreshore and made occasional notes in a pocket book. Then, he knelt and scooped a sample of soil into a small plastic container.

They had started already! He was one of them. He must be associated with Prestige Developments. As required under legislation, an Environmental Impact Study would have to be prepared before the proposal could be considered by the planning authorities. He must be collating preliminary data to support that report.

Alyssa's anger bubbled to the surface. Her safety in that situation no longer concerned her. She burst through the vegetation previously screening her and started down the slope towards the stooping figure. He glanced up from his squatting position, his eyebrows raised in surprise as he noted her approach. The broad shoulders straightened, and he waited curiously as she drew up before him.

"You're wasting your time. We're a close-knit community around here, and we neither want nor need your fancy development!"

Now only one eyebrow was raised as the cool, green eyes regarded her with sardonic amusement. "Is that so?" he drawled.

Alyssa's head jerked up and for the first time, she actually looked at the man. With arrogant stance, he towered over her, the sun behind him casting his features into silhouette. She felt at a distinct disadvantage as she screwed her eyes up and squinted at him. She could sense as much as see the impression of solidity he exuded. *Bully. I guess he thinks he can intimidate people as well as desecrate the environment. Well, think again, mate!*

"Don't just take my word for it," she re-joined tartly. "The reaction you'll get from the people who love this area will be unified—as you'll find out if you continue with this unacceptable proposal."

"And you are…?"

"I'm Alyssa Finchley, and I'm a lawyer. I have all the resources and contacts to challenge any development on this parcel of land."

"Lawyer… hmm. I didn't think there were any in Sandy Bay."

He took a couple of steps towards a backpack he'd left on the ground. When he bent down to pick it up, and stood again, she could see him more clearly. He looked vaguely familiar, but that was silly. She didn't know anyone from Prestige Developments. She didn't even know many people in Sandy Bay, besides the neighbours either side of Seaclusion Cottage. Paul and Jacinta lived in Pt Reilly. If he was familiar with lawyers, he must often find himself in legal strife. The thought did not make her think kindly of him.

She regarded him with a moue of distaste. "This is one lawyer you don't know, but soon will if you continue with this project. That's a promise."

To her annoyance, he grinned. "It seems you have a habit of making assumptions and flying off the handle. I thought lawyers were more circumspect. Seems I was wrong."

What did he mean, *you have a habit?* He knew nothing about her. He had no reason to smirk at her like that either. She couldn't stand smug, arrogant men. Men in general were not in her good books at the moment, so this one had better watch his step. In her current mood, she could take to his balls with a bolt cutter and toss both them and him off the cliff. On second thoughts, he looked too solid for her to do that, but she could still tear strips off him if he got too close.

"No doubt you'll learn how far off the handle I can fly." She gave him a withering smile. "I'd give your bosses a warning, if I were you."

She whirled around and stomped back to where she'd left her book and chair. Reading no longer had its appeal, not there, anyway. She would retreat to the deck of the cottage. It took her less time than usual climbing the path back to Seaclusion. The flush of anger she felt gave her new found energy. The fight had begun.

She looked back from the sanctuary of the deck, and saw the man picking his way through the bushes to where he had parked his car. He threw his backpack onto the back seat and opened the driver's door. He knew he was being watched. Before he slid behind the wheel, he looked up in her direction and gave a wave. The nerve of the man. Alyssa turned away, not wanting any semblance of connection with him.

Only then did she remember why he had seemed familiar. He was the man she'd seen on her previous visit to Sandy Bay. He was the father of the boy who had stepped onto the road in the path of her car. He couldn't even look after his own son.

Max watched the woman push her way through the overgrown path. Belligerent female. When he'd first seen her, she was sitting back with her face lifted to the sun with the breeze whisking small tendrils of hair around her face like a soft halo. The image reminded him of Botticelli – an angel in the bush. Disturbing a woman by herself in a secluded location was a definite no-no. He'd crept away quietly and got on with his work.

Her sudden emergence from the shrubbery took him by surprise. The verbal attack and the underlying fury jogged his memory. She was the same woman who had berated him when Jeremy ran onto the road. She obviously didn't have small children. If she did, she'd know how unpredictable they could be, particularly an active kid like Jeremy. She'd been quick to make assumptions on that occasion too.

He saw her head towards Seaclusion Cottage. Seclusion was something she needed. With a tongue like that, she wasn't safe to unleash on the community, not in Sandy Bay anyway. Feisty women didn't usually disturb his work. That was fortunate, as he didn't need the drama of women in his life. He and Jeremy got along just fine without additional complications. Hopefully, this contract would be completed soon, and he wouldn't connect with her after that. She would be Prestige Development's problem.

He saw her emerge on the deck after she had reached the cottage, looking down over the tract of land he was surveying. The thought that he was being spied on and watched made him uncomfortable. He'd done as much as he intended to that afternoon, and he needed to pick up Jeremy from the sitter. He slung his backpack over a shoulder and walked back to where he'd parked the car.

Without looking too obviously, he saw that she still watched from her vantage point. Perversity made him wave. If he'd been close enough, he would have winked as well.

3 – Where There's a Will

ALYSSA TRIED TO not let the encounter spoil her weekend, but her anger hadn't subsided by the time she arrived at work the following Monday morning. She needed to talk to Paul. There had to be a way to challenge the development, and he would know if there were any regional protest groups. She didn't want to come across to the locals as a blow-in from the city who was a know-all, but her legal knowledge could surely be to some advantage.

"Morning. How was your weekend?"

Jodie was disgustingly cheerful for the start of the week. Alyssa gave a non-committal nod and mumbled an answer before dumping her laptop in her office and continuing down to the kitchen. She needed a coffee before engaging in casual chat. Paul had beaten her to it. With mug in hand, he stood gazing out the kitchen window.

"Wishing you were still out there?" she asked.

"I've already been for a surf this morning. If I get up early enough, I can catch a few waves before coming to work."

She shivered. "That's dedication. Isn't the water freezing?" She grabbed her mug from the cupboard and placed it under the spout for the coffee machine. The first decision of the day was deciding what coffee selection to make.

Paul didn't take his gaze off the scene outside. They had a view of the coast line stretching back towards Sandy Bay from that side of the office. "A wet suit takes care of that. It's cool enough to remind you you're alive, but not so cold as to freeze your balls off."

"Lucky, I don't have any," she replied tartly. She joined him at the window with mug in hand, inhaling the rich aroma before she took a sip. "It's a lovely view. Pity it's under threat."

Paul looked at her enquiringly. "What do you mean?"

"My godmother told me that Prestige Developments are negotiating a deal with the council on the community land along the cliff top. If successful, they intend building a resort on that land."

"I've heard about it. The proposal has created local rumbles," he admitted, "but there was nothing detailed in the minutes of the council meetings."

"Discussions of that nature are always held 'in confidence'. There would be no mention of the deal in the minutes that are publicly available." Alyssa turned to face him. "Anyway, something is definitely happening. On Saturday, I saw a man prowling around the site and taking soil samples. It's my guess he was part of the development team."

He lifted his eyebrows in surprise. "That's a worry if your assumptions are correct. The community will be up in arms at losing access to that land."

28

"That's what I thought. If it's not too presumptuous of me, I'd like to get involved in the community action. Do you know who I should contact?"

"Leave it with me; I'll put out feelers." Paul walked as far as the kitchen door before pausing and glancing back over his shoulder. "A friend is coming in later to organise his will. I have to get the Fletcher Contract finished today. Can you look after Max?"

"I haven't done a will for a while, but I'm sure I can handle it. I'm available for the more complicated work as well, don't forget."

"Of course. This job is more of a favour to a mate. Look after him."

Paul left her to her coffee. She gave a regretful look at the view through the window and carried her mug back to her office. Time pressure wasn't quite the same as in the city, but there were still files waiting for her attention. She worked steadily until ten thirty, when Jodie popped her head around the edge of her office door.

"Max Saunders is here to see you. Paul said you'd be handling this client."

"Sure. Give me a moment and I'll come and collect him." Alyssa tidied her desk and saved the file she'd been working on. She opened her notebook to a blank page and placed her fountain pen by its side. Everything looked in order.

The client had ignored the reception seating on offer and stood at the front window, hands behind his back, watching the street activity outside.

"Mr Saunders?"

He turned. The surprise she saw on his face must have reflected the expression on her own. She hadn't expected this. The man in front of her was the man she'd encountered on the headland. She'd been about to extend her hand, but quickly changed her mind. Fraternising with the enemy was bad enough, but that didn't mean she had to be sociable.

"Please come this way."

She led him back to her office and indicated that he should take a seat. She used her most officious tone. "I understand you need to draft a will."

"Yes, and guardianship papers. I want to make arrangements for my son in the event something happens to me."

"Very sensible. We'll deal with the will first, and then the guardianship document." She uncapped her fountain pen. "Full name, date of birth, occupation and address?"

He supplied the details. *Environmental Scientist; thought so.*

"Beneficiaries?"

"My son, obviously—Jeremy Michael Saunders, and my sister. Eloise Margaret Saunders."

"And your partner, Jeremy's mother?"

"Deceased. Cancer. Two years ago." His curt tone was devoid of emotion.

Alyssa glanced up from her notes. She hadn't expected that response. The green eyes were veiled and his face took on a set look, not inviting further questions. What was there to ask, anyway? It must have been a dreadful time, with a small child too.

"I'm sorry to hear that. Under those circumstances, it's even more important that provision is made for your son."

He inclined his head. "That's why I'm here."

A memory flooded over her and with it a flush of embarrassment. She had yelled at him that day when his son had dashed onto the road. *Your wife shouldn't let either of you out without a leash.* Of all tactless things to say… not that she could have known of his situation. That didn't change how mortified she felt. Perhaps he'd been right the other day when he'd accused her of making assumptions. The look he now gave her was knowing, as though aware of the thoughts flashing through her mind.

She scrambled mentally to retrieve the situation. "Would you like a cup of tea or coffee?" Normally, she would have made that offer at the beginning of the meeting.

He folded his arms. "No, I just want to get this over and done with."

"Of course. Can you give me a summary of your assets, and how you propose to distribute them?"

The remainder of the meeting was businesslike, but cordial. Alyssa took notes, and made suggestions about how his assets might best be put in a trust for the benefit of his son, with varying actions happening according to the age of the child, should his father die.

"I recommend you talk to your financial planner about the structures that will give you the best result. You need funds to be released to pay for the maintenance of your son, but also want to preserve some money for when he comes of age."

"I'll do that. Do you need anything else from me?"

"If I do, I'll let you know. I'll prepare a draft according to the information you've given me and email it to you"

"Thank you. I'll get back to you promptly with any comments." He collected the few notes he'd spread on her desk and stood. "If there's anything you need before then, don't hesitate to contact me."

Alyssa moved to the door and opened it. "Before you go, I should warn you that I can't let a client relationship stand in the way of my opposition to the proposed development on the Council land. It's zoned community land for a very good reason. It's for the benefit of the whole community, not just a privileged few."

She didn't mean to sound hostile, but it probably came across that way. He lifted one eyebrow a fraction as he turned to face her. In that enforced proximity as they stood by the door, she couldn't help but be aware of his physical presence. In her high heels, she was almost as tall as him. This time, he extended his hand and she felt obliged to take it. His palm generated warmth and his handshake was firm. For a milli-second, a tingling response shot up her spine, disappearing as quickly as it came. Perhaps he had squeezed a nerve.

"I agree," he said.

Now it was her turn to tilt her head and look enquiringly.

"That land is an important community resource. I wouldn't get side-tracked by all the rumours if I were you."

He didn't wait for a response, but headed down the passage. He waved to Jodie in reception and then was gone. Alyssa returned to her desk and sat. She didn't resume working for a while, but pondered what he'd said and what it might mean. It highlighted the need for research, rumours as well as facts.

***

So, she's the new lawyer in town. When Paul had told him a lawyer from the city was joining the firm, he'd assumed it would be a man. More fool him. Of all people, it had to be Angel from the headland. Not that she was angelic. Far from it, even if she did have that mass of unruly curls. She might even be appealing if she smiled. From what he'd seen, that rarely happened.

At least she came across as professional and knowledgeable. He'd seen her eyes widen slightly when he mentioned that Clara had died. That news always invoked a reaction in people, usually expressions of sympathy and invitations to dinner, as though he and Jeremy needed help and feeding, but her response had been purely professional.

Under those circumstances, it's even more important that provision is made for your son.

Her approach was a relief in a way; he didn't have to deal with rote sympathy and she didn't ask him endless questions about Clara and her death. All he wanted was to ensure that his son was adequately provided for, and to be able to get on with their lives without outside interference. Assuming she did a good job, that would be one less concern on his mind. There were plenty more when it came to being a single dad.

***

Alyssa hadn't cut all ties with the city. Her best friend, Charlotte rang her that evening for a chat.

"How's the new job? You're living the dream, having a sea-change. Perhaps I should come down and check it out."

"You're welcome any time, you know that. There's plenty of room in the house. Graphic designers can work from anywhere, so you could easily make the change if you wanted."

"Sure, but can you get good coffee, and what's the night life like? Any good men around?"

"Good coffee, yes and I have absolutely no interest at all in the men. I can live without them and for very good reason."

"You just picked a dud this time round, that's all. Not every man is like Phillip."

"I don't care. I'm not interested." *Not even in men with green eyes and thick luxurious hair that many women would die for.*

"Speaking of Phillip," Charlotte began hesitantly, "I ran into him at a friend's barbecue over the weekend."

Uh, oh. Alyssa's gut told her that this was in part the reason for the call. "And…?"

"Did you know that some woman has moved into the house with him?"

Alyssa's blood pressure zoomed from zero to boiling in an instant. "My house? Are you saying he's moved some other woman into my house?"

"It's his house too, isn't it? Didn't you buy it together?"

"No, we didn't. It's in my name only."

"I'm sorry… I didn't know whether to tell you or not. I didn't want to upset you."

"You absolutely did the right thing. I had a right to know."

The conversation petered out after that. Alyssa was too furious to talk much and Charlotte chattered for a while about mutual acquaintances, but then claimed things to do before the night was over.

"I'll come and see you soon, I promise. Bye-ee."

Alyssa sat for a while after disconnecting the call, phone still in hand. Charlotte's news had taken her by surprise. It was incredibly quick for Phillip to move on, and the fact that he had established another serious relationship so quickly could only mean one thing. He had been seeing the other woman for a while behind her back. She had been so naïve not to pick up on it earlier.

Tiger wound himself around her legs, purring loudly. Usually that was a precursor to a demand for food, but he had already been fed. He was just seeking attention. Perhaps she would scorn men forever and become a career-driven cat-lady. She scooped the cat up and hugged him tightly, burying her face in his soft fur until he squeaked and struggled to be set free.

"Are you rejecting me as well, Tiger? This is not my day." Once released from her grasp, the cat settled on her lap. It was as Mary had warned her. Tiger was an independent cat who interacted with people on his terms. That night he slept on her bed.

By the time daylight cracked through the curtains, Alyssa felt a total wreck. She'd found it impossible to let go of the thought of some other woman in the bed she'd shared with Phillip. Her mind raced and she'd hardly slept if at all, leaving her with a throbbing headache. On top of that, a fat cat lay across her legs most of the night. She rolled over occasionally to dislodge him, but after a while, he crept back again.

She swung her legs over the side of the bed and padded out to the kitchen and put the kettle on. Her mug still sat on the benchtop. In the early hours, she'd heated some milk in the hope that it would help her to sleep. If it did, it wasn't for very long. Now she made herself a cup of tea, and reviewed the thought jags she'd had through the night.

She had loved that house. It wasn't new when she'd bought it, but was structurally sound and in good condition. She'd upgraded the bathroom and kitchen, and values in the area had appreciated nicely, taking her property along with them. Having a place of her own meant independence.

She and Phillip had been together for a couple of years before he moved in with her, and that had been a major step. His one-bedroom unit was only rented, and had been too small to accommodate them both comfortably, particularly when they occasionally worked from home. It had made sense for him to move in with her instead, given the understanding that they were together for the long haul and at some stage, would get married. Although the property remained in her name, they had treated it as their house, and Phillip had helped with some of the renovations.

That was in the past. Her memories in the house were sullied and it was time to move on. Agonising over the decision had contributed to her sleepless night, but in the harsh light of day it seemed to be the right one. She would sell the house. When she returned to Adelaide, whenever that might be, she could buy another, or even purchase an investment property now while she lived in Sandy Bay.

The re-purchasing decision could wait. The first step was to evict Phillip. She would ring him first and follow up with a formal notice to quit. When she'd fled the house, her thoughts had been confused. There'd been anger, humiliation, disbelief and embarrassment; embarrassment that she'd been cuckolded in this way.

Initially, she didn't want to see him again, but she had to return the next day to collect more clothes and a few other bits and pieces. Phillip had apologised and promised it wouldn't happen again. Part of her wanted to believe him, and to keep hold of their future together. It was in that frame of mind she agreed he could stay on in the house while she was in Sandy Bay. He agreed to pay rent, and she told herself it made sense to have someone looking after the place.

She never expected him to treat her as such a fool. Had she ever really known him? She had to call him now while her resolve was strong. The longer she delayed, the more she would agonise over it. She had to cut Phillip totally from her life.

She showered first and chose her clothes for the day. She dressed in what she had always thought of as her power suit; a charcoal grey pencil skirt topped with a red jacket. She put on stockings and high heels and applied her make-up, more than usual for Sandy Bay. Her whole image communicated that she meant business. Phillip wouldn't be able to see it, but she could feel it and that would give her the confidence for the conversation she dreaded.

His mobile number was on speed dial on her phone, and taking a seat in the dining room, where the window looked out over the bay, she pressed the keys.

"Alyssa? This is early."

Hearing that voice usually made her light up inside. Not today. He sounded tired. Someone keeping him up, perhaps? The thought hardened her resolve.

"I'm selling the house. I'll make arrangements today to list it with an agent. You have until the end of the month to vacate."

"What? Fuck! And good morning to you, too. What's brought this on? I thought we agreed I could stay while you worked in your little coastal retreat."

"That was before I knew you were shacked up with some skank in my house. I didn't agree to that."

"You left. You can't expect me not to move on. It's not as if you said you wanted to come back."

"You're a self-centred, two-timing prick, Phillip. I assume you were seeing this woman for some time before I caught you in the act. That was so tacky."

His silence said it all.

"I'll be back next weekend to clear out the house. You can keep the bed and anything that's yours. What I don't need or don't give away, I'll put into storage. I'd appreciate it if you were somewhere else while I'm there."

"I didn't expect you to be such a bitch."

"Phillip, I haven't even started." She disconnected the call, and to her dismay, her eyes welled and tears trickled down her face. She wasn't crying for Phillip... not for him. She grieved the loss of her dreams; a supportive partner, a future together and perhaps one day a child. Was that too much to ask?

A box of tissues sat on the kitchen counter and she pulled out a handful and blew her nose and blotted her face. If it wasn't for the fact that she may still have some arrangements to make with him, she would have blocked Phillip's number. He was a non-person as far as she was concerned.

4 – The Dinner Party

ALYSSA LOOKED FORWARD to dinner with Paul and Jacinta. She had dined with them on a previous visit to Pt Reilly. They were superb cooks and conversationalists, and she knew she was in for great evening on every level. She considered the forthcoming meal as she stood first on one foot, then the other, contemplating her open wardrobe. Eating so much was not obligatory, but perhaps an outfit which didn't fit too snugly around the waist would be a good idea.

Pulling the jersey knit over her head of tumbled curls, she smoothed it over her hips, turning to check the draping in the mirror. The French-blue colour suited her, and it was one of her favourite dresses. She'd been told the colour accentuated the indigo blue of her eyes, and that was another plus.

Some thirty minutes later, Alyssa pulled up in front of the House on the Hill, as she liked to call it. Paul and Jacinta lived high above the harbour in Pt Reilly on an allotment that was never likely to be overlooked by neighbours. They had designed it themselves to take maximum advantage of the glorious view it offered, with large picture windows and minimal curtaining so they didn't feel too removed from the environment.

"Alyssa, you look lovely… as usual!"

"You look good yourself. I love the earrings you're wearing."

Jacinta fingered the art deco drop hanging from one ear. "They were an inheritance from my aunt. I like to wear them on special occasions." Giving her guest a warm hug, she relieved her of the chocolate gift, with murmurings of "how wicked!" that fooled neither of them, and directed her out onto the balcony.

"Go on through while I get you a drink. Paul and Max are already out there."

Did I hear right? Alyssa paused and looked enquiringly at her host. "Max?"

"Oh, didn't I tell you? I meant to, I'm sure. Paul and Max have known each other since they were kids. He's doing some work in the area at the moment and the two of them have been catching up on old times."

Alyssa caught her breath and closed her eyes briefly in dismay. Surely not *the* Max, the one who had turned up in her office earlier in the week? She would have to be on her best behaviour. If Jacinta noticed her reaction, she didn't mention it.

"Here's your drink. You might as well take it out there yourself while I take refills for the men."

Alyssa followed Jacinta out into the balmy evening. The two men leaned over the balcony railing, taking in the spectacular view it gave them. Over their shoulders, Alyssa had a brief glimpse of fishing boats returning to harbour before the low murmuring ceased and the reclining forms straightened and turned around.

After smiling a greeting to Paul, she turned to acknowledge his guest. She hadn't been mistaken. It was him. He looked just as astonished to see her.

"Well, well! It's the fiery angel of the bush. I hope you're not going to attack me this evening as well."

"Attack is too strong a word, isn't it? I merely wanted to make you understand that your development isn't wanted." She maintained a stiffly polite attitude, and her eyes slid over him and focused on the scene behind. Her dismissiveness said more than any words could.

Paul and Jacinta exchanged looks, clearly intrigued. Paul shook his head.

"Max—I didn't realise you two had met outside of the office? What's this about an angel? There are many descriptive terms I've heard applied to Alyssa, but angelic certainly isn't one of them."

Jacinta playfully swiped her husband's arm. "Paul, just what are you inferring? Pay no attention Alyssa; he's only teasing. So, when did you two meet? You've not been in town very long."

Alyssa took a deep breath. The situation was unexpected, but that was no reason why this man should tarnish an evening that by past experience, should be stimulating and enjoyable.

"We don't exactly know each other, outside of the office connection of course, but I never discuss client matters. I noticed your friend taking photographs and making notes down at the headland last Saturday, and took the opportunity to make him aware this crazy development of his is not wanted by the local community."

Paul's face lit up in an aha moment. "So that was who you saw. I should have guessed when you mentioned it. Being Monday morning, my mind was elsewhere."

Jacinta erupted in a peal of laughter. "His development! But Max, didn't you explain?"

"We didn't exactly pass the time of day, and as for explanations, I wasn't asked for any, let alone given the opportunity to offer them." This last comment was delivered with a wry smirk.

Why is it I've got this nasty feeling I've put my foot in it somehow? With the benefit of the balcony lighting, she covertly studied Max Saunders. He was tall enough to have a commanding presence, and quite broad across the shoulders. His informal attire of jeans and open-necked shirt was more casual than when he'd been in her office, though not out of place in this setting,

He had a shock of wheat-gold hair atop clear green eyes, and a decisive jaw line. He could even be considered attractive, if that combination appealed, and it didn't. It was as far removed from Phillip and his suave city appearance as was possible to get. On the other hand, that relationship hadn't ended so well. Instead of Phillip's usual Aramis after shave, she picked up a slight hint of citrus and something else. Sandalwood perhaps?

Alyssa felt herself flush when she realised not only was she staring, but she had been caught in the act. One eyebrow twitched slightly and she noticed the hint of a smirk. He probably thought she fancied him. Fat chance.

"Formal introductions… how remis of us," interjected Paul. "Alyssa, I would like you to meet an old friend from school days, Max Saunders. Max, you are looking at one of the most knowledgeable commercial lawyers ever employed in Pt Reilly. She usually works in the big end of town, with all the high flyers in the corporate world.

Max inclined his head in acknowledgement. "I'm impressed. I'm fortunate you consented to draft my will."

Paul gestured expansively with his bottle of beer. "Mind you, Alyssa, Max is no slouch either when it comes to the credit stakes. He's made quite a success out of his own environmental consultancy."

I'm sure he has. If it's such a success, he can just take his consultancy successfully elsewhere.

"Alyssa, you'd make a hopeless poker player. Your face reflects every thought." Jacinta passed around the nibbles with a smirk. "Actually, you and Max have a bit in common. He's an environmental scientist and here to do the first stage of an Environmental Impact Study and I believe you were heavily involved in that recent case representing the fishing community after the oil spill in the Port River."

"It's not just me working on this project. We work as a team in my line of work, each according to his or her speciality," interrupted Max. "You were right in assuming I was at the headland area because of the proposed resort development, but not as the developer, I'm afraid. The business may be doing well, but not that well."

He paused, looking out towards the shoreline, still visible beneath them. "In this instance, I've been engaged to provide a study as part of the pre-requisites to obtaining development approval. I was taking a few photos, taking soil samples, making notes, getting a feel for the site and its topography, and observing what there is in the way of flora and fauna."

"How much influence does this study of yours have on whether or not the project proceeds?"

"That depends. As the name suggests, we're considering the impact the project will have on the environment. If the detrimental factors outweigh those that have little or no impact, then it is likely development approval won't be given. Of course, the developer may assess those impacts and make relevant changes so the negative factors are removed or ameliorated."

"You mean the work you do can be used to make sure the application is successful." Alyssa didn't disguise her antagonism. Her eyes blazed with such intensity that the others were left in no doubt they were teetering on the edge of an eruption of volcanic proportions.

My God, what am I doing? This is not the time or place to be getting on my hobby horse. "Sorry, I didn't come here to start a crusade about this project. I get carried away sometimes."

"Okay, grub's up," Jacinta interjected brightly. "Hurry up. I've slaved over this meal for hours and I'll not have it go cold while you lot stand out here chatting."

Releasing her pent-up breath, Alyssa took her place at the table, not altogether pleased to be seated next to Max, but graciously realizing there wasn't much alternative. She

45

enjoyed the dinner, but with such good hosts, it was difficult not to. The mood relaxed, and Alyssa found herself laughing on several occasions. Once, she looked up and found Max's eyes fixed steadily on her. She found the inscrutable look disconcerting. It was impossible to tell what was on his mind.

"More wine?" Max held up the bottle, looking at her with eyebrows raised.

She held her hand over her glass. "I'm driving, so I won't. I'd love some water though."

He picked up the jug, and as he held out a tumbler, his hand brushed against hers. She tried suppress the mild electric jolt that teased her body at his touch. She glanced at him in surprise. An odd look flashed across his face before he began pouring his own glass of water. Perhaps she had imagined it.

She focussed instead on the remains of the meal in front of her. "You two have excelled yourselves again. I'll have to brush up my culinary skills if I stay in Sandy Bay for much longer."

Jacinta smiled, but Alyssa noticed that Paul took her hand and gave it a small squeeze. They made a good team. She glanced away, focussing on the dark swells of the ocean visible through the picture windows and suppressing the unexpected surge of jealousy. Phillip had never shown his support for her in that way. The more she thought about it, much of their relationship had been about her supporting him.

"I'd be surprised if you didn't have some prize recipes in your repertoire," Max said. "I have the impression you excel at most things you put your mind to."

"I do a great line in cinnamon toast. With my working schedule, it was easier to eat out, or order in." She smiled lightly to indicate she was downplaying her cooking. Phillip had preferred eating at the restaurant of the moment when they entertained.

The evening passed more convivially than it had started, and Alyssa was surprised when she checked the time. They had adjourned to the balcony again for coffee and a liqueur. She downed the last of her coffee and placed her cup on an adjacent coffee table.

"Thank you for a fabulous evening, but it's time I headed for home. I try to fit in a walk early in the mornings before work, and I'll never get up in time if I stay much longer."

Max also placed his cup on the table. "I agree, it has been most enjoyable." He turned to Alyssa. "Can I trouble you for a lift back to Sandy Bay? I left my car and the child seat with the baby sitter, and caught a taxi here."

It was no trouble to her, but Alyssa wished it was possible to refuse. She had no desire to prolong her association with Max Saunders other than in a professional capacity. That feeling was not helped when, as they were leaving, Jacinta gave her a wink and subtle nudge. Alyssa chose to ignore both with the disdain they deserved.

Max belted himself into the front seat of her car and gave her his address. "Thanks for this. I hope it doesn't take you too far out of your way?"

"Not at all. Nowhere is too far out of the way in the Bay."

His question gave Alyssa an idea. He wasn't taking her out of her way, but perhaps she could take him out of his. She swung off the highway onto a lesser road. Max didn't say anything, but risked a sideways glance, made as if to speak, and then stayed silent.

She pulled up close to where they'd met the previous Saturday. As she turned the engine off, silence surrounded them. "Listen, just listen," she said.

Alyssa pressed the button winding down the car windows. Faintly at first, and then more loudly as they tuned into the sound, waves could be heard lapping on the shore. A symphony of night creatures called, chirped and croaked in the bush around them.

"I won't keep you long, but I had to bring you here. It's so beautiful and peaceful but as you can hear, it's very much alive."

She climbed out of the car and he followed suit. They walked down the slope a little, and then stood quietly. A gentle breeze washed over them, doing nothing to dispel the natural scents of the bush.

"This area is public property, and the locals have always had the run of this stretch of headland. It's communal land for everyone, whether ratepayer or not. It's land no-one should own, but perhaps those who care can be guardians or custodians for the benefit of everyone."

She took a step closer and placed a hand on his arm. His expression was enigmatic in the shadowed moonlight. For a moment, she thought he was about to kiss her. His head inclined towards her and she was sure she could feel the heat of his body. Her gut lurched in shock or anticipation; she wasn't sure which. Nervously, she licked her lips before pushing the thought aside and rushing to speak.

"You do understand don't you that this is a special place?" The sea breeze picked up tendrils of hair, whipping them around her face in a medusa-like halo. "I thought if I explained properly, you would understand what I was saying. Max, you can't possibly let them go ahead with this project."

"Alas, and I thought it was my company you craved out here at night," he mocked. He reached out and brushed a strand of hair from her eyes, bringing a quick flush to her cheeks.

"Don't make fun of me. I'm being serious. You'll tell the Prestige Developments that this site is not appropriate for their resort, won't you?"

"Angel, I can't do that. I'm employed to undertake an Environmental Empact Study, not to give judgemental advice. That would be unprofessional. All I can do is report on the impacts as I find them, as impartially as possible, and the decisions are made by others after assessment of my report."

"Impartial? That's a laugh! Everyone knows these studies are slanted the way the client wants them to go. If you don't discourage them, you'll sound the death knoll for this beautiful area."

The earlier moment of intimacy shattered. Glaring with undisguised hostility, Alyssa turned and ran back to the car. "Perhaps you can continue your rational assessment here, because I won't take you any further."

He stood motionless as she fled, and didn't try to follow. A wave of guilt washed over her as she accelerated down the road with a shower of small stones in her wake. He only had a ten-minute walk back to his house, and it was a moonlit night. Even so, she knew she had behaved badly. It was his fault anyway. Why didn't he see how his work contributed to the loss of the land?

~

Max watched the tail-lights disappear around a bend, and with a sigh, turned back to contemplate the darkened panorama before him. Paul hadn't mentioned who else had been invited to dinner. In the absence of information, he'd assumed he was the only guest. Her appearance had been a surprise, though not unwelcome.

After witnessing her antagonism the day he'd first encountered her, he'd been surprised that she'd maintained her professional façade during his legal consultation. He'd never seen anyone flare up as quickly as she did, but Alyssa was clearly passionate about matters close to her heart.

It wasn't far for him to walk home, but he wanted to sit for a while. He found a large flattish rock, and perched on it, drawing his jacket tightly around him. Looking up the hill, he saw the lights of Alyssa's car as she drove up the driveway to Seaclusion Cottage. An outside light flicked on as she left the car and walked across the deck. She stood for a moment, looking out over the scene below and towards the ocean. He knew she couldn't to see him, but still felt like a voyeur. Then she turned and went inside, and the light on the deck was extinguished.

In spite of her accusations, he wholeheartedly agreed with her. It would be a tragedy if this land was developed. His firm needed the contract though and he wasn't about to get Prestige Developments offside, nor the Council for that matter. He and his team would undertake thorough research and would report the facts in an impartial manner. It wasn't like making representation in a court of law, whereby each side tried to present the facts in a way that best supported their case. Her accusation about bias made him snort. The law was not squeaky clean.

Other thoughts kept him sitting out there in the dark. The project didn't dominate his life. For two years, it had just been him and Jeremy. They were a team. Clara's illness had been swift and brutal, and they both grieved terribly. He'd thought he and Clara would be together until old and grey. Life had other plans.

Another relationship didn't interest him. He didn't need that complication in his life. That's why it had been such a shock when he found himself reaching out to touch Alyssa. With moonlight highlighting those auburn curls, he'd momentarily forgotten why they were there. He hadn't touched a woman for some time, and hadn't expected those feelings to be stirred. The visual effect had been the same when he'd first seen her with the sun on her face. Both times she'd been hostile to him. Would that always be the effect he had on women?

Bloody hell – the sitter! He'd told her he wouldn't be late. He couldn't afford to get her offside, not in a small town like Sandy Bay. He stood and dusted off the seat of his trousers and set off along the rough path, grateful that the intermittent moonlight was sufficient to light his way. At one point, a small animal scurried across the path in front of him, but too quickly to tell what it was. He would stake out the site to monitor the known fauna, but not tonight. Tonight, he was going home.

5 – Selling the House

SHE'D BEHAVED BADLY. She knew that. A client too. What had she been thinking? Silly question. She hadn't thought. She'd fired up like a cracker on New Year's Eve. When Paul learned of what she'd done, there were bound to be repercussions.

Alyssa wandered out onto the deck, clasping her morning cuppa between her hands. She wore a kimono robe over her pyjamas, and the morning breeze caught it, billowing the robe behind her. Leaning against the balustrade and standing high above the bay like this made her feel like the figurehead on the bow of a ship.

She looked down over the headland, half expecting to still see Max sitting forlornly in the bushes. He wasn't, so hopefully he made his way home without too much trouble. She sighed, rubbing her eyes as though that would impart clarity on the issue. She had to apologise to him, but that could wait for a more reasonable time.

The still water beyond the shore mirrored glorious sunrise colours. Golden peachy hues, tinged with pinks stretched before her. The jetty reached out into the water, providing a man-made element to the scene. She knew that fishermen would be sitting patiently at the railings, hoping to snare some crabs or perhaps a squid. Even from this distance, she could see a lone pelican sitting on the jetty railing. A view like this would calm the spirits of even the most troubled soul. On impulse, she slipped inside and fetched her phone. She took several photos, showing the headland in the foreground and the mirrored sea and sky behind it.

Tiger wound his sleek body around her legs, reminding her of his presence. She bent down and scratched the cat's head, resulting in a loud chirruping purr.

"Food coming up, Tiger. Bowl of milk and some fishy food?" The cat gave a small meow of acknowledgment and she moved back inside to make her breakfast and get ready for work.

For once she was the first one in the office. She fired up the coffee machine and poured herself a heart-starter before heading back to her room. With a few clicks on her laptop, she opened the folder containing Max's files. There were a couple of points she wanted to check in the draft of the will and she reviewed those first then read through the document one last time. Satisfied with the final draft, she attached it to an email and clicked send.

That left the apology. Scanning through his file, she found where she had noted his contact details and picked up her phone. She took a deep breath and dialled. It was answered after only a couple of rings.

"Hello?"

He sounded abrupt and he didn't even know who it was. Bad night? "Max, it's Alyssa. Two things—I've just forwarded a draft of your will. Review it when you have time and get back to me with any comments or questions."

She paused, but there was no response from him.

"Secondly, I need to apologise. Losing my cool and driving off last night was unforgivable. I hope you got home safely."

"There were no vampires, bunyips or werewolves around so yes, I did. The walk was a refreshing end to the evening." His tone was icily polite.

"Dad, who's on the phone?"

Alyssa heard the small voice in the background.

"Shush, Jeremy. Don't interrupt while I'm talking."

The voice persisted. "Is that the dragon lady?"

"Jeremy, finish your breakfast!"

Alyssa heard a door shut. Presumably, Max had moved to another room. "You're obviously busy so I'll let you go. When you're ready, make an appointment with the office to execute your will and have it witnessed. Densley and Partners will keep a copy on file."

After disconnecting the call, she sat nursing her head in her hands. Dragon lady! That was how Max had described her to his son. She'd probably been called many things in the past, but usually it was couched in terms like dedicated, persistent, professional even but never dragon lady—until now!

Max's opinion of her shouldn't matter, but it rankled. After the humiliation of Phillip two-timing her, the reference cut deep. Would all men hold her in such low regard? She thought of how those green eyes had engaged with her over dinner the previous night. For a while, she had forgotten where and how she'd met him and had really enjoyed the evening. She reached for the dregs of her coffee, now disgustingly cold. She would focus on her work from now on.

***

This would be a day of physical activity. She pulled on an old pair of jeans and secured her hair back with a hair tie. Traffic travelled from the city towards Sandy Bay on weekends, so Alyssa knew that in travelling in the opposite direction, she would make good time back to the house in Adelaide. She left a bit later than she initially intended, but pottered around feeding Tiger, watering the pot plants and sweeping up fallen leaves before she left. She didn't normally procrastinate, but then she didn't usually make such life-determining decisions. Selling the house rated highly on the stress-inducing scale.

By the time she eased the car out of the drive and onto the road leading through the main part of town, it was already ten o'clock. Saturday morning shoppers were out in force, and the early tourists cruised slowly as they looked for convenient parking bays. She used the time paused at a pedestrian crossing to turn on the car radio, selecting the Classical FM station. She didn't recognise the music, but hoped it would ease the tension of her drive.

As the last stragglers dashed over the crossing, Alyssa glanced at the tables set up on the footpath outside one of the cafés. Max sat there with his son and someone else; a rather attractive woman. As she watched, the woman reached over the table and laid a hand on Max's arm in a gesture of familiarity. No longer mourning his wife then. The blast of a horn from the vehicle behind her alerted her that the road ahead was clear and cars were banked up behind her.

She accelerated away, glad that Max hadn't noticed her. The tableau she had just witnessed made her feel like a peeping tom. Max might have thought she was spying on him if he'd seen her gawking from the car. He hadn't given the impression of being involved with anyone, but even so, it was none of her business. The last thing she needed was to be exposed to someone else's relationship. Her own was bad enough.

Little more than an hour later, she pulled into the driveway of the house with a heavy heart. Perhaps it was a reflection of her mood, but the property had a sombre vibe. The garden was neat and tidy, but she couldn't shake off the feeling of sadness and that coloured her perception. Someone must have applied a grey filter over the day. She returned a wave from a neighbour, but hurried inside before she could be waylaid by casual conversation. They would all learn soon enough what was happening.

She shut the front door and leaned against it, listening to the house. It was unnervingly silent. Not even a ticking clock. Looking around, she could see by the personal possessions that were strewn around, that Phillip was still in residence, but in keeping with her instructions, he'd gone out for the day. There was no point in stalling. She had to make the most of her time. She wandered through each room, assessing what was there, what she would take and what she would leave behind. Some furniture could be stored, but other items she would probably donate to a refugee association.

The last place she wanted to go to was the bedroom, but to get to the ensuite, she had to do that. She found nothing of importance—a half-empty bottle of shampoo, a few cotton buds and the remnants of make-up she no longer used. She swept the lot into a rubbish bag. Phillip's toiletries were there, and two toothbrushes as well. She recognised Phillip's, but not the other. On impulse, she swept that into the rubbish bag as well.

Ignoring the bed, she opened the door to the walk-in wardrobe. Most of the stuff was Phillip's, but she still found a couple of pairs of shoes she only wore occasionally, some handbags and other accessories. They hadn't been high on her list of priorities when she'd left the house, but now for convenience she shoveled them all into another rubbish bag and left it by the front door.

The rubbish bags were useful. She'd brought a new packet with her. By the time the real estate agent arrived she had cleaned out the linen press and started on the kitchen. She heard the car pull up and when she peeked out the front window, saw the driver climbing out of his Audi, parked behind hers in the driveway.

Mark Pedlar was a fashionably-dressed young man, without being too sharp. He stood for a moment, hands on hips and surveying the exterior of the house. Alyssa had met him a couple of times when he had acted on behalf of clients of hers, and had been drawn to his open smile and easy-going personality. Results counted though, and she had also been impressed by his level of professionalism and his track record in achieving good sales on behalf of his clients.

On hearing the front door open, he strode towards her with hand outstretched, accompanied by his trademark smile. "Alyssa… great to see you again. You're looking well."

Liar. I feel like shit and it must be showing. "Glad you could make time for me on the weekend, Mark. I need to sell my house and need advice on current value and the state of the market."

His hand felt smooth and warm to her touch, and she caught a hint of spicy cologne. He turned that high-wattage smile on her and she felt heat rise on her cheeks in response. He probably did that to all his female clients, but she was inwardly bemused at her flustered reaction. In previous interactions with Mark, she'd been dressed in business attire and in a professional setting. Her ripped jeans and loosely dragged back hair fell short of that standard.

She wished she'd at least coated her lashes with mascara, even knowing the thought was silly. She wanted him to sell her house, not flirt with her. He could save the charisma for all the female prospective buyers who came to inspect the property. It was flattering though to think that men other than Phillip could be interested in her.

Mark stayed for the best part of an hour, noting the key features of the property and explaining the various marketing options and associated costs. They agreed on a program which suited her timeframe, budget, and aspirations.

"I think you've answered all my questions," Alyssa said after examining the clauses in the agency agreement.

"Do you need time to think about this? I can give you a few days to think it over if you prefer."

"Give me your pen. There's nothing to think about. I need this to be over and done with." She took his pen and signed and dated the document, throwing the pen down on the table when she finished. "Done. Up to you now to get me a good price."

"The market dictates the price, but I'll guarantee you to get the best result possible."

Alyssa had expected to feel devastated after arranging the sale, but instead felt the opposite. The sense of freedom was unexpected but liberating. She could leave the relationship in the past where it belonged, and instead focus on the future. While she worked in Sandy Bay, she could use her time to brainstorm her next steps in life; where she lived, where she worked… Perhaps she could travel. She'd never taken a gap year and maybe now was the time—after Mary returned and her contract with Densley and Partners terminated.

The improved frame of mind made the rest of the day easier to manage. She sifted, sorted, labelled and packed. Some boxes and bags went into her car, and she dragged others into the spare room downstairs to be picked up later by a removal firm. It could go into storage with the furniture she decided to keep.

Evening approached by the time she completed the tasks she had set herself. Initially, she panicked, thinking that Phillip would be back soon, but then realized that she didn't care. Phillip was no longer part of the equation.

6 – Launching the Campaign

NIGHT SETTLED AS she drove back to Sandy Bay. She flicked through the radio stations on the car audio system until she found one with easy-listening music that suited her mood. Her thoughts returned to the events of the day and what next. It would take a while for the house to sell, but she could still make positive changes in her life before that. She could join a gym, perhaps join the book club Jacinta had mentioned, and definitely plan an overseas holiday. Antarctica perhaps, or Tuscany? There were so many options.

In the meantime, she would put some energy into the campaign to stop the clifftop development. There were arguments both for and against the project. A resort development could bring affluent tourists to the town, and there were many business owners who thought that would be a good thing. If she was going to convince the public, the Council and the Developer that the proposal should not go ahead, then she needed to present a good reason why. With so many conservation groups working on different projects around the state, it was always possible that people would become blasé about yet another development proposal.

Inspiration came from an unexpected source; a phone call from Mary not long after she arrived home.

"Are you settled in? How are you and Tiger getting on?"

"He's fine. Typical bloke, really. Keep him fed and keep up with the belly rubs and he's as happy as a pig in whatever."

Mary laughed. "Nothing's changed then. I won't keep you long—these international calls cost a fortune. I've got a favour to ask."

"Sure. Ask away."

"An old friend, Delia Kennett, is visiting Sandy Bay. She grew up here but now works with the Dept of Environment and Sustainability in the city. Delia's a botanical scientist, and is doing some local research. She probably doesn't know many people in town now. I'm sorry not to be there for her. Can you invite her to dinner one night or take her to lunch?"

"Sure. Give me her contact details and I'll follow up with her. She sounds interesting. How are the travels going?"

"Fabulous so far. Don't know why I didn't do this years ago. Have to go, but I'll email you."

Alyssa made a mental note not to delay her own travel plans too long. Why should Mary have all the fun?

When the email with Delia's details arrived, Alyssa rang and invited her to dinner.

"It will just be something simple. Mary's sorry she's not here but asked me to invite you to Seaclusion."

"She has a lovely house. I've visited a few times over the years. I've fond memories of evening drinks out on the deck."

"Subject to the weather, I'm sure we can do that again. Shall we make it Wednesday evening?"

Delia turned out to be younger than Alyssa had expected. She'd assumed the woman was the same vintage as Mary, but apparently, they had met at a conference and established their links to the Bay. As Delia explained, she was born and raised in Sandy Bay, but moved to the city in search of work and adventure. Her parents had died recently, but her work as a botanist brought her back to the region on a regular basis. In fact, she had just published a book titled 'Native Vegetation in Coastal Regions'.

Delia placed a book on the table. "Can I leave this with you for Mary? I received a box of books from the publisher just before I left Adelaide. They're hot off the press."

Alyssa picked up the book and rifled through the pages. It still had that new book smell. The picture plates depicted plants and flowers of the region, many of which she recognised.

"I've seen that one; it's down on the headland."

"I'll come back in daylight and check it out. It's indigenous to this area. With increasing housing development, there aren't many undisturbed growing areas."

"Have you had an official book launch?"

"Not even an un-official one. I haven't had time to organise it and the publisher hasn't seemed interested either. I gather that publicity is mostly up to the author these days."

Alyssa stared at her, her brain whirring. "Are you here for a while? This is a fabulous opportunity. I'd love to organise an event for you."

Delia sounded surprised. "Would there be enough interest?"

"I'm sure there would. The timing couldn't be better. I'm drumming up opposition to the proposed resort development down on the headland and launching your book there would give the campaign a focus."

Alyssa's brain went into overdrive as she realised what a brilliant opportunity Delia had provided. She could give a practical demonstration on plant identification and explain that if the development went ahead, rare plants with such valuable properties could be under permanent threat. It took a bit of persuasion and another glass of Chablis to get Delia fully on-board. She fully supported the issues outlined by Alyssa, but as she explained, she had never been one to seek the spotlight.

"It'll be easy—you just have to talk about your book and the plants in the area and I'll do the rest. Say you'll do it… please?"

"If you really think people would be interested… if it helps to protect that area of native vegetation… well, okay. I'll do it."

"Great. I'll organise it for the weekend after next. You're a godsend. It will benefit you and the community too."

The following morning brought a flurry of activity. Alyssa knew there was no time to waste if she wanted to muster support in the campaign to stop the development. She needed manpower, publicity, political support, and focused community attention.

Using local contacts provided to her by Paul, she organised a communication tree, with those people broadcasting the news of the event to others in their network.

She made sure to notify council of her plans, in deference to the fact the land was council-owned. She followed up with community leaders, political representatives, and the local newspaper and radio station. She even managed to talk to the producer for a popular current event television program, but they were waiting to see if the issue developed wider interest before pursuing it further.

Notice was short, but Alyssa drummed up support, coordinated press releases, and in conjunction with a local book shop, arranged delivery of copies of the book for sale on the day. They agreed to run the sales table.

The gods must have been smiling for the day was beautiful, organisational activities went smoothly and a good crowd turned up, including the press. Paul and Jacinta were there of course, although Alyssa avoided prolonged conversation in case Jacinta asked her anything about the lift home she had given Max on the evening of the dinner.

Her stomach clenched with unaccustomed nerves as she surveyed the assembling crowd. This was different to a court room, and even then, she rarely appeared in court. Her arguments were mostly presented in a board room. She climbed a small, rocky outcrop that gave her clear view over the gathering, cleared her throat, and launched into her welcoming speech before introducing Delia.

The botanist wasn't the only speaker. She had persuaded a local historian to talk about the regional history, and Aunt Rosemary, an aboriginal elder who had known the area as a child in more traditional days, told the crowd about the significance of the land to her people.

All that remained was the summing up. Alyssa surveyed the crowd. She caught her breath when she saw Max standing at the back. His height and thatch of blond hair made him easy to spot. As she watched, he exchanged a few words with council staff, who were also at the rear of the crowd. No doubt they were assessing her arguments and the level of community opposition.

She faltered for a moment, and the brief silence caught his attention. He looked directly at her, eyebrows slightly raised. Well, let him listen!

"Residents of Sandy Bay—what you have heard today has been both interesting and informative, but you had better listen well and take lots of photographs, because if the resort development goes ahead, it will no longer be available in this form to you, to your children, or to their children. Is that what you want?"

She projected so that her voice carried over the crowd, and her words were punctuated by murmurings and comments by those present. "I urge you all to sign the petition that's circulating, and let your local councillor know about your opposition to this project. Only if you speak up will the council know community views. Copies of Delia Kennett's book are also on sale from the table on my right. Thank you all for coming."

People gathered around the sales table to examine and hopefully buy a copy of the book, and a volunteer collected signatures on a petition to be presented to Council. Alyssa stood back, watching the activity. Delia had been cornered by a couple of residents wanting to discuss aspects of her book, and Alyssa was ready to rescue her if necessary.

"Well done. You pulled together an interesting event."

Alyssa tensed. She knew who it would be without bothering to turn around. *Not bad for a dragon lady, you mean?* "That was my intention."

She turned to face him, unsure what his attitude to her would be. Jeremy was with him. He gripped his father's hand, staring at her uncertainly. Father and son looked very alike. Jeremy would be a hot package when he was older. She pushed the thought aside and focused on Max.

"I didn't expect to see you here." To her surprise, he smiled at her.

"Why not? Contrary to what you seem to think, I'm not a proponent of the development. As I've tried to explain before, I have a job to do here. I'll be as thorough as I can in presenting a report that is professional, and gives an accurate summary of the environmental situation. The presentation this morning has been highly relevant. I'd like to speak further to the author." He nodded towards the people thrusting books at Delia to be autographed. "When she's free, I'll set up a time to have a more detailed discussion."

Alyssa shoved back a strand of hair that flopped over her eyes. She was irrationally pleased to see him, even knowing that was stupid. It had crossed her mind that he might not want to speak to her again after she had abandoned him. She could introduce him to Delia. That would go part way towards erasing her feelings of guilt.

"Come with me. I'll introduce you."

They pushed through the crowd. Aunt Rosemary was surrounded by a group of children, telling them a story about the first nations people who lived and fished in the area in earlier times. Jeremy's attention was drawn to the cluster of kids, and after a whispered appeal to his father, he dashed off to join his friends.

Alyssa eased Delia aside from those clustered around her, and introduced her to Max.

"Delia, Max is the person I mentioned who is undertaking an environmental assessment of the area. He just heard you speak and wanted to ask you a few questions."

Delia smiled politely, with her head tilted to one side as she looked up at him. Max launched into a series of questions about the site coverage of the local plants, and Alyssa zoned out. Best she left them to it and networked within the crowd instead. She saw Ben Benedict, one of the local building contractors hovering to one side of the conversation. She wasn't sure who he was waiting for, Delia or Max, but he might have a wait ahead of him if those two got engrossed in detailed discussion.

While addressing the crowd, she'd spied the mayor and council CEO standing on the outskirts, and wanted to speak to them before they left. She'd seen the mayor about town. The portly man was an accountant in his day job and from his weekly column in the local paper, Alyssa had the impression he considered himself an expert on most things to do with the town. She saw him nudge the CEO on her approach. The thought that they considered the need to be on guard in her presence amused her.

"Gentlemen—thanks for coming. It's been a good turn-out. The locals have certainly expressed their concern about the potential loss land from community use."

The mayor puffed out his cheeks before replying. "An interesting morning, but not all the facts were presented. I wouldn't expect a recent blow-in to understand the economic needs of the local community."

Blow-in? You presumptive arsehole. Alyssa smiled sweetly. "I've been coming to the Bay for years, and this site in particular is close to my heart. If the Council develops an effective Economic Development Plan that addresses the needs of the region, madcap schemes like resorts for the rich on community land wouldn't rate a mention. It's a lazy approach, don't you think?"

The man's eyes widened and he drew a breath as though about to give strong retort. The CEO placed a hand on the other man's arm to halt the anticipated response.

"The organisers of this meeting have made a lot of assumptions. Council is only engaged in preliminary discussions. No decisions have been made."

"Hopefully, today has given you a better understanding of local antipathy then. If you want to put together a community-based working party to workshop an Economic Development Plan for the town, I'm happy to volunteer my services. I might have some useful contacts and experience."

She didn't wait for a response, but spun on her heel and headed back to where Max still spoke to Delia. Jacinta cut her off before she reached them. She dug Alyssa in the ribs with a manicured finger.

"What's this I hear about you and Max having an altercation on the way home the other night?"

"Don't believe everything you hear. This town relies too much on gossip."

"Is that so?" Jacinta's reply was delivered in an arch tone. "I don't know about that, but there's little that happens around here that goes without notice." She regarded Alyssa speculatively. "You wouldn't make a bad couple, if only you both could see it."

"There's no point in matchmaking. Even if we were on the same wavelength in relation to this development, the last thing I need is another man in my life. I haven't fully extricated myself from the last one. I'm learning to appreciate the joys of single living."

"He was a prick. You're better off without him, but you will form a new relationship. You can't bury yourself away forever with just a cat for company."

Alyssa snorted. "Tiger's a mighty handsome cat. He and I get along just fine."

She saw Max wander over to the story-telling group to retrieve his son. He must have finished his conversation with Delia. With a seemingly reluctant Jeremy in tow, he scanned the crowd before locking eyes with her, and dragging his son in their direction. He had one of Delia's books clutched under an arm.

"I hoped I'd still catch you," he said. "We're about to head home, but tomorrow, I'm setting up a camera in this area to check for nocturnal wild-life. Something scuttled past me the other night in the dark. Could have just been a rabbit, but the cameras will help with identification. You might like to join me when I set up the equipment."

"Me? Why would I do that?"

He shrugged. "You might like to learn more about the process we use in undertaking an environmental assessment."

Jacinta broke into the conversation. "That would be so interesting Max. You should go, Alyssa; who knows what you might learn. Paul is waving at me, so I have to go. See you both later." She rose on tiptoe and kissed Max on the cheek and after taking a few steps out of his line of vision, turned and gave Alyssa a cheeky wink.

Alyssa thought quickly. She would find the survey interesting, but didn't want to appear too eager. Besides… if she saw how he operated, she might pick up some useful information for the campaign.

"When do you plan on doing this?"

"I'll be back here about ten tomorrow morning to scope out potential sites and set the cameras up."

He glanced up to where Seaclusion overlooked the site. "With the view you have from up there, you'll be able to see if anyone interferes with them, so having you involved is a win."

"Okay, I'll join you, but only because I want to learn more about the area. This doesn't mean that I'm softening my stance towards the development."

"I wouldn't expect anything less." He laid a hand on his son's shoulder. "We can go now." As they moved towards the edge of the crowd, he glanced back in her direction. "See you tomorrow."

She was good. She had known how to work the crowd. Max had watched the people who turned up for the event and noticed they listened intently. Alyssa had them in the palm of her hand. Full marks to her for pulling it together. Some of those gathered used their phones to take pictures, but none that he saw were scrolling or being disengaged, and that spoke volumes.

She presented herself as 'one of them', not some hot-shot lawyer from the city. Her head of rust-coloured curls flew free, and being dressed in jeans, Katmandu vest and sturdy walking shoes, she could easily pass for one of the local women seen most days of the week in the town's main street.

The pang of recognition had hit him unexpectedly. Alyssa looked like Clara—not the mirror image, but dressed in a carefree fashion with an attitude advising anyone who cared that she was comfortable and confident in her own skin. That in itself was sexy. He didn't welcome the thought. He didn't need that sort of complication in his life. All he wanted was for this project to proceed smoothly, without unnecessary angst from the community.

The idea came to him after his conversation with Delia. He wanted to survey the nocturnal wildlife in the area, and to do that, he had to set up some cameras. He would do it when there were no people around. It would be an expensive disaster if cameras were stolen or vandalized.

He looked up at the house on the cliff, the house overlooking the headland. As Alyssa had mentioned during her speech, she had grown up with the view she was so desperate to protect. She lived in an ideal location to monitor activity on the headland. The solution was obvious. He would invite her to join him when he set up the cameras. She would get a better understanding of his work, and might agree to keep an eye on the installation. It was a win-win as far as he was concerned. For him, anyway.

7 – Secret Picnic Places

HOW LONG SINCE she'd slept in this late? In her drowsy state, she could easily snuggle down for longer, After the frenetic activity in organizing the protest meeting, she needed time to unwind and just 'be'. Alyssa rolled over, resulting in a protesting yowl from the lump leaning against her leg. It moved, and Tiger stalked the length of her prone body to stare into her face. He bumped the top of her nose with his, leaving a damp spot behind.

"Is that a wake-up call? If you were a well-trained cat, you would have brought me a cup of tea in bed."

The cat mewed softly in response and stared at her expectantly.

"Okay, okay… I'm getting up. The service here is lousy."

She threw back the covers and slid out of bed, stretching before padding to the window and throwing back the curtains. She loved the view, no matter what the weather conditions, and looked forward to the surprise revealed each morning. The day looked indecisive. Gone was yesterday's sunshine; low-slung clouds hovered on the horizon, and a murky-blue sea surged beneath. Seagulls flew in widening arcs, floating on the updrafts for a while before swooping back down to the beach below.

"Breakfast inside today," Alyssa advised the cat. "That weather doesn't look pleasant."

After dressing, she set out food for Tiger in the kitchen, and took a bowl of muesli topped with banana into the dining room. Here, she could look out over the coast in comfort. She had just poured herself a coffee, when she noticed movement on the headland below.

Who's down there this morning? It looks like… oh my God… Max! I'd forgotten.

She downed her coffee in a couple of scalding gulps, then grabbed her jacket and house keys. As she paused on the deck to shrug her arms into the jacket, she saw Max look up towards her. She gave him a wave to indicate she was on her way and headed for the steps leading down towards the front of the property and the path leading to the clifftop.

An icy wind swept up from the sea, and danced around the foliage. Alyssa zipped her jacket up to her neck, and wished she had thought to grab a scarf and beanie as well. She was surprised to see Jeremy squatting beside Max, chattering about all the animals they were likely to see.

"Will there be kangaroos?"

"Not here, mate. They haven't been found around here in years. Maybe some small marsupials, that the local cats haven't eaten."

Max didn't look at her as she approached, but stood again with hands on hips surveying the vegetation around him. "I thought you might have forgotten, or decided not to come."

And good morning to you, too. "Not at all," she fibbed. "I had some domestic duties to attend to, but hadn't forgotten." Well, feeding Tiger counted for something. She didn't want to sound too keen, but she really was interested. She hadn't seen anyone set up this sort of surveillance, and who knows what it might disclose that supported her stance on the project?

"Aren't you going to introduce me to your son?" Alyssa asked pointedly. *And don't dare refer to me as the dragon lady.*

"Of course. Alyssa, this is my son, Jeremy." Max gestured towards Seaclusion. "Alyssa lives in the house up the hill, and is going to help us set up the cameras today. She can keep an eye on them from up there as well as me from the ground."

The boy assessed her with green eyes that were a mirror of his father's. She had no idea what he was thinking, but it was a while before he spoke. "Do you spy on people?"

"Of course not; not on purpose. I have a good view over the coast from up there, and can also see over this parcel of land. My friends and I used to play down here when I was a kid. We had cubbies and secret places where we used to have picnics. It was our special playground."

"What did you eat?"

Trust a boy to be interested in food. "Apples, sandwiches or biscuits. Sometimes my godmother would give me some cake to share around. I can show you one of our picnic places later—after we've finished the work your dad has to do."

"Good idea. Work first, play later." Max hefted his backpack onto his shoulder. "First, we have to look for any obvious signs of animal activity, such as burrows, footprints or scats. Then we can select the best locations for the cameras. I'd like to set up three at least; maybe more."

He considered the open space around them. "Did you see any animal life on these fabulous expeditions when you were a kid?"

"We weren't here at night, and were probably too noisy through the day. There were plenty of birds and small reptiles. There could have been various small marsupials. I would have dismissed them as being rats or rabbits. There were lots of bunnies around."

"And you might be right, but I need to check it out. We'll head along the cliff face first, and then work our way back through the middle."

Alyssa noted that Max had morphed into operational-mode. The surveillance work was his turf and he was directing events. This new side of him was thought-provoking. She risked a sideways glance when she thought he wasn't looking. He wore jeans, which fitted his derriere to perfection. *Nice.* His broad shoulders were encased in a leather jacket, quite different to the style Phillip would have opted for. He looked dependable, if you liked that sort of man.

On second thoughts, were any men really dependable? She would consider that question another time. Right now, there were small, furry animals to think about.

"Would a waterhole be of interest?" Alyssa asked. "It's not very big, a small rockpool at best and sometimes it dries up."

"Why didn't you tell me before? Of course, it's of interest. Where is it?"

She pointed back along the cliff-face behind them. "It's down that way. There is a small gully with a minor waterway following its path when it rains. Some of the water gets caught in a rocky basin, forming the pool. It dries up in the peak of summer, but it's amazing how the area re-vitalizes in the wetter months. We used to catch tadpoles there, so the frogs magically appeared with the water, or so we thought."

Max did smile at that comment and for the first time that day, looked directly at her. "It's amazing the changes a bit of water can bring about. It sounds promising, but we'll head down this way first and work our way back to your rockpool."

He set off, pushing his way through the vegetation, with Jeremy close behind and Alyssa bringing up the rear. Occasionally he stopped and crouched down to examine the ground or to lift some of the low branches aside. Jeremy crouched beside him, aping his father's actions and asking lots of questions.

"When will we find an animal, Dad?"

"We won't, not today. They'll hide when they hear us and only come out at night. That's why we need the cameras—to take pictures and prove they live here."

His patience with his son impressed Alyssa. He explained to the boy what signs he was looking for and what they might mean. She wished there had been someone like Max to teach her these things when she was small, but her father rarely came down to Sandy Bay, and after her parents separated, he never came again. Another reason to distrust men. They leave you when you need them most.

The cameras were motion-activated, so would only take photos when someone or something crossed the sensor beam. Max positioned two in locations of his choice. He straightened from his crouching position after setting up the second.

"Hopefully those units are concealed well-enough that a stray hiker isn't going to find them. You'd better lead us to your miraculous waterhole. It sounds like a potential location."

This time, Alyssa took the lead, pushing her way through the shrubbery towards the gully and its associated waterway. She hadn't visited the exact location in some years, and found herself hoping it was still the same. She would feel such a fraud if she led Max on a wild goose chase. Sometimes childhood memories magnified themselves with time. She would feel cheated if the waterhole was merely a slight dip in the rocks, or even if it didn't exist anymore.

She paused uncertainly, looking back towards Seaclusion and then towards the edge of the cliff. She charted the route in her mind, thinking back to when she explored as a child.

"Do you know where you're going?"

Max's sardonic tone irked her. "Of course, I do. It's a while since I've been here, that's all. I'm working out the best route to take."

"Dad, don't ask silly questions."

Alyssa smiled to herself at Jeremy's reproachful tone. She hadn't expected the boy to come to her defense. The closer they got, the more she recognised the topography and surrounds. The gully was as she remembered, though not as steep. The pool still existed, though was currently a stagnant bowl of water, with green slime around the edges.

"I'm sorry, this doesn't look very enticing."

"It might not be to you, but to a small marsupial it could be just what it needs. I'll set up a camera here, and then we can think about the final location."

He went about his business in what was now a practiced routine. Jeremy happily poked in the water with a long stick whilst Max selected the best location and mounted the camera. The case was in camouflage colours, so hopefully it wouldn't attract attention from either two or four-legged activity.

"You can see what a great play area this was for kids," Alyssa said with pointed reference to Jeremy. "I think these days it's called expressive play, or something like that. Then it was just called keeping out of our parent's hair and having fun."

"I'm not arguing with you. I'm sure you had a great time."

"Is this where you had picnics?" Jeremy asked.

"Not specifically. Those places were closer to the main path. When your dad has set up the last camera, I'll show you."

By unspoken agreement, the last location was further away from the cliff face and closer to the location in which they had first met that morning. Max selected the site, took a photo to remind himself later where he'd left the camera, and zipped up his backpack.

"Finished for now. Picnic spots it is. Then lunch, I think."

"We had a few favourite haunts," Alyssa said, "but I'll take you to the one that's closest. I was there recently, so I know it's not overgrown and is still accessible."

She led them to the clearing where she had settled with her chair and book on her first weekend back in Sandy Bay. "We liked it here because we could still see the water, but we weren't visible from the main path across the headland. Also, it wasn't too far if we needed to dash home for more supplies."

"More…?" Jeremy screwed up his face.

"More food. We went through a lot of it. We dragged down some old wooden boxes and used those as chairs. One of the kids brought down an old tarp and we rigged up a bit of a canopy so we had shelter as well."

"What happened to them?"

"No idea. It was a few years ago now. I'm not sure if kids do that sort of thing now."

"I like picnics," Jeremy said, looking hopefully at his father.

"That you do. Today though, we're having lunch at home. The weather's not great for picnics, and we didn't bring any food."

Max turned to Alyssa. "See what you've done? I now have juvenile expectations to deal with."

She laughed. "That's what being a father's all about." She smiled at the boy. "I'm sure your dad will bring you back another day, Jeremy."

Max gave her a look indicating that sitting in the scrub playing at picnics was not his idea of fun, but she ignored it. A wicked part of her even smirked inwardly at the prospect. "I think we're done for now, so I'll head back home. Don't tell anyone about the picnic place, Jeremy. That's a secret."

The small boy looked at her solemnly, eyes wide, and clutched his father's hand. "Can I come back again?"

"If your father brings, you I'm sure you can."

"Another day, perhaps," Max said. "In the meantime, I'll see you back here around nine tonight?"

"Me… back here? What for?"

"I want to check the cameras. I'll make sure they're working and that none have disappeared or been kicked over. If there's any nocturnal activity, it will start around dusk so we can check if any images have been captured. I'll bring a couple of headlamps, so we'll be able to see."

"That will be a bit late for Jeremy."

"He'll stay with his grandparents. It will just be you and me."

As he strapped Jeremy into his car seat, Max eyed Alyssa's figure as she made her way back up the hill towards Seaclusion. *Nice bum.* Not that he would let her know that. Being a lawyer, she'd probably have him up on some sort of harassment charge. The last thing he needed in his life now were more dramas. He and Jeremy needed stability as much as anything.

As they pulled up in the driveway to his house, another car pulled in behind them. A look in his rear vision mirror told him who it was. Emma. He closed his eyes briefly, then put a smile on his face and stepped out of the car.

"Hi! I come bearing gifts. Looks like I timed my arrival perfectly."

"You did indeed. I'll just get Jeremy out of the car." Max opened the rear door and after unclipping the seatbelt, stood back so Jeremy could clamber out.

"Is that Aunty Emma? Has she brought something for us?"

"The answer is yes, and yes."

"Goody."

Max sighed. He hated his son thinking that people visiting meant treats for him, but it was difficult to prevent others from spoiling the boy.

Emma gave Jeremy an awkward one-handed hug, and deposited a plastic container in Max's hands. The bottom was slightly warm, indicating the contents were not long out of the oven.

"I thought you might like a contribution towards lunchboxes and morning tea."

"Thank you, but you know you don't have to feed us. We get by quite well."

"I know you do, but I promised Clara I'd look out for you both and that's what I'm doing. It's not much, and anyway, who else am I going to bake for? Jeremy loves my biscuits, don't you sweetie?"

Max knew she would do whatever she wanted, no matter what he said. "Would you like a cup of coffee? I'm about to put the kettle on. We can test your latest culinary delights."

"Well… all right. I won't stay long, but Jeremy can tell me what he's been up to this week, and you can fill me in on what's happening with the resort development."

She followed them inside, and Jeremy promptly showed her his latest drawings, and demonstrated his transformer toy. Emma made all the right noises and complimented the child until Max presented her with a mug of coffee. It only took

Jeremy a microsecond to notice that his father had put some of the biscuits on a plate.

"Can I have one?"

"Sure, just one or you won't eat your lunch."

"We could take some back to the secret place and have a picnic."

"Secret place? What's this about?"

"I can't tell you, cos it's a secret. The lady said so."

Emma paused with the cup halfway to her lips and looked enquiringly at Max. "That sounds intriguing."

"We met up with Alyssa Finchley this morning. She lives in Seaclusion, overlooking the headland. She came with us while we set up some cameras in the scrub to record any wildlife activity. She'll keep an eye on it from her vantage point. She also showed Jeremy a place where she and young friends used to hang out when they were kids."

"That was nice of her. Of course, we can have a picnic anytime. It doesn't have to be a secret."

Jeremy eyed off another biscuit. "This one does."

Emma reached out and ran her hand over Jeremy's head. "His hair is getting rather long. Do you want me to take him to the hairdresser?"

"Thanks, but we'll probably drop into the local barber together… a bit of father-son bonding, you know."

The dubious look on Emma's face indicated that suggestion didn't sit comfortably with her, but there weren't any valid objections. A man could take his son to get a haircut. She picked up her keys.

"I'll be off then. I'll pick up the container another time. Let me know if you need anything."

Max showed her to the door. "We'll be fine, but thanks. I don't expect you to go out of your way for us like you do."

"What else are friends for? You should both come over to dinner one evening through the week. I'll give you a call."

He shut the door behind her with some relief. If only he didn't feel so guilty. He appreciated everything she did for them both, but he also knew there was an ulterior motive, and he wasn't ready to go there. Emma was a friend—Clara's friend—and he still regarded her as off-limits. He would never have made a move while Clara was alive, and wouldn't do so now.

It was a day for being indulged. Clara's parents had invited them to dinner that evening. Jeremy was staying the night. It was easier that he slept over, rather than Max coming back late to pick him up. Gordon and Rose loved having their grandson stay over, and would take him more often if they could.

Jeremy gave them a version of the day's activities, in no particular order, talking about the secret, the rockpool, and the various types of animals they might see, some of which Max had never heard of. He also mentioned Emma coming to visit, bringing yummy biscuits.

"Goodness, you won't have room for ice cream then," his grandmother teased.

"I will," he assured her, "cos ice cream just slides down and doesn't take up much room."

Later, as Jeremy sat reading a book with his grandfather, Rose had a quiet word with Max. "You know, we don't expect you to remain on your own for the rest of your life, and Clara wouldn't have wanted that either. We won't object if you form a new relationship. It would be good for both of you."

"Rose, I'm not even thinking about that. If you've got Emma in mind, she's just a good friend, Clara's friend. It's best we keep it that way."

"You don't have to rush into things. You might feel differently after a while. All I ask is that if you do form a new relationship, we don't lose contact with our grandson. He means so much to us."

Max seized her in a hug. "Rose, you and Gordon mean so much to us too, and you've helped in providing Jeremy with some normality in his life. Of course, you wouldn't lose contact. I'd see to that."

He glanced at his watch. "I've got to check the cameras soon so I have to go. I'll be back early in the morning to get Jeremy."

He let his son know he was leaving, and strode out to the car. The clouds from earlier in the day had cleared. That was good news. A clear sky might encourage more nocturnal activity. He drove towards the headland with thoughts turning to the woman who should be waiting for him.

8 – Nocturnal adventures

A TEASING BREEZE swept over the clifftop from the beach below and challenged anyone within cooee. Clouds that had obscured the sky during the day had disappeared, leaving a crisp, starry night. The walk down to the headland from Seaclusion in the dark became a reasonable proposition. Once her eyes adjusted to the night, Alyssa found she could see quite well.

The lack of cloud also increased the chill factor. She pulled her beanie over her ears. *That wind must come directly from the South Pole. Remind me again why I agreed to this caper? I should have worn some gloves.*

Beyond the call of a night bird, and the rhythmic surging of the waves, all was quiet. If there were any animals scarpering around, they did so silently. Max hadn't arrived. She hoped she hadn't made a mistake about the time. It could have been scary, alone in the dark, but she made her way to a large rock she knew provided a great sitting option. Seated there, she had an unobscured view over the coast and the pulsing sea below. She could also see if anyone approached.

The breeze carried a briny smell. It was the smell of her childhood, and time spent on the beach. Alyssa shoved her hands in her jacket pockets for warmth, and thought of earlier night-time walks with her parents. She had loved the feeling of security, walking between them, sometimes clasping a hand and sometimes running ahead into the dark, giggling at admonitions not to go too far. That was before she was aware of the tensions between her parents and the dramas that followed.

A light swung over the headland, and when she looked over her shoulder, she saw the headlights of an approaching car. As it neared, she heard the soft purring of the motor. It stopped in the parking area just off the access road, then a car door slammed. Max. With her adjusted night vision, she saw him standing beside the vehicle, hands on hips and looking around. He was probably looking for her, but she knew he wouldn't see her where she sat.

That invisibility meant she could observe him without him being aware of her scrutiny. Moonlight picked out the thick waves of his hair, unusually abundant for a man. Alyssa wondered what it would be like to run her hands through it, then chastised herself for being irrational. That was an involvement that was so not going to happen.

It amused her to see Max peering into the dark. Alyssa took pity on him, and uncurling herself from her rocky seat, walked towards him.

"I'm here."

Max swung around at her words, with his hand shielding his eyes as he peered into the night. "Alyssa? That's you?"

"Who else would it be out here at this time of night? I've been sitting here enjoying the solitude."

"Sorry to disturb your peace. After we check the equipment, you can go back to communing with nature, or whatever it was you were doing." His tone indicated he wasn't at all sorry.

She yawned in response. "I think by then it will be time for bed. Just me, I mean. My bed. I wasn't issuing an invitation."

Max raised his eyebrows. Even in the dim light, she could see the bemused expression on his face. He pursed his lips as though about to make a comment, but instead shook his head slightly and rummaged in his backpack.

That was a really stupid comment. Note to self: don't mention beds in future.

Max extracted a couple of head lamps from inside his pack and held one out to her. "If you put this on, we can make a start. It helps to keep hands free. I hope we can find all the sites in the dark."

"Shouldn't be too hard. Even if I didn't know the way, you took photos of each location. The first camera is along the cliff edge behind us." She dropped her voice level to just above a whisper. "Do we have to speak quietly, or even not at all?"

"Quietly, and to a minimum until we've checked them all. I'll let you lead the way, since you obviously know where you're going."

They set off in single file following a narrow path. Foliage grabbed at their legs as they passed, making rustling noises.

Any small mammals would still hear them coming. Cold bit at her cheeks, and Alyssa could feel that the moist tip of her nose was threatening to drip. She tried to sniff quietly while she rummaged in a coat pocket for a tissue. She didn't want Max to accuse her of frightening the furry creatures away.

For an uncertain moment, she thought they must have passed the spot, but when she looked around more carefully, they stood only a couple of metres from the installation. Max directed his torchlight around the area, checking for activity before dropping to his haunches and checking the camera was where he left it. Nothing had disturbed it and when tested, the equipment appeared to be operating normally.

They made the rounds of the other cameras, following the same procedure. The rockpool was quiet, but still magical as the light reflected off the surface of the water. They could almost have entered a parallel universe, with the unworldly atmosphere that surrounded them. Alyssa gasped in delight.

"It's quite surreal, isn't it? Almost dreamlike. I half expect to encounter a water nymph or perhaps a dryad or two."

Max looked at her oddly. "That's more imaginative than I expected from a lawyer." He gestured towards the water. "There won't be much activity at this time of night. Typically, animals come to water to drink at dawn and dusk. I'll know for sure what's happened when I examine the SD Card." He gave her a sardonic look. "Perhaps we'll find one of those dryads."

"Are you going to take it out now?" The prospect of seeing those visitors made her curious.

"No, I'll leave everything set up for three nights, and then I'll check the cards. My purpose in coming back tonight is to check that the cameras are still in position and operating." He gave her a cheeky grin. "Bringing you with me on this exercise means that you can see for yourself what I'm doing. Who better than a lawyer to oversee the process?"

"You don't need me to verify what you're doing. You've told me often enough that you don't have a stake in this project, other than being engaged to provide consultancy services. I assume you have your own checks and balances regarding your work."

After another thirty minutes, they were back at their starting point. All the cameras appeared to be operational and none had been tampered with. They didn't see any animals, but as Max said, that didn't mean there weren't any.

"They would have heard us coming from miles off. Their little whiskers would twitch and they'd make the smart decision to stay put until we were out of the way."

"You're probably right, but I hoped we'd see something anyway. I've never explored the area at night, beyond the one overnight camp and the hoots and shrieks of us kids would have frightened away drop bears and dingoes, let alone small marsupials."

"You weren't concerned being down by yourself at night? I should have picked you up on my way here."

"Don't be silly. It's a moonlit night, and it's hardly a dangerous location. Besides, I had a great vantage point looking out over the coast. I saw you long before you saw me. I'll show you, unless you're in a hurry to get home."

"Jeremy's with his grandparents, so no rush. I'd like to see your vantage point, as you call it."

Alyssa led the way again, pushing her way through the over-grown path until it opened out to an area on the clifftop. The flat stone stood out in stark relief against the seascape. "You can see a lot from here. There's a good view along the shoreline, and then looking back the other way, I could see if anyone approached. The rock has long been one of my thinking places. If I need to sit for a while and just gel while I sort out the problems of the universe, this is a great place to do that.'

"Did you sort out any problems tonight?"

"Sometimes, it's a good place to just sit. That's what I did tonight."

"If I promise I won't intrude anytime that you're here, is it okay if sometimes I come here and *just sit* as well?"

"Of course." Alyssa parked herself on the rock and patted the stony surface beside her. "You can *just sit* now if you like."

He perched beside her, gingerly at first and then settled back on the smooth surface of the hunk of sandstone. The close proximity to his body put her senses on high alert. His leather jacket smelt of conditioner and it reminded her of a coat her father used to wear. Her father never aroused such tingly feelings though.

To distract herself, she pointed out towards the ocean. "Given it's a moonlit night, you can see along towards Port Reilly. The lights of the town are in the distance, if you look carefully."

She glanced back at him, and saw that he wasn't looking at Port Reilly at all. He was looking at her. He was close enough that she could have run her hands through his hair, but that wasn't all she noticed. Those well-shaped lips that would be the envy of any woman were tantalizingly close to hers. The urge to kiss them was almost irresistible.

Don't do this to yourself. Just don't. She closed her eyes, shutting out the temptation. His leather jacket creaked at he moved, and then she felt it— a feather-light kiss that brushed the surface of her mouth. Startled into opening her eyes, she looked into his. She knew them to be green, but now they just looked broodingly enigmatic.

"Sorry," he said. "I blame the moonlight. It's bathing your face in such a soft glow— you looked like one of your dryads with your face tilted up to bask in the light. I'm sorry," he said again. "I overstepped the line."

She regarded him silently for a moment, her glance drifting down from his eyes to those delectable lips and back again. Acting before she even understood what she was doing, Alyssa reached up and wrapped an arm around the back of his neck. Drawing his head towards hers, she kissed him, gently at first and then with a heat and passion that took her by surprise.

This is a crazy idea. What possessed me to ask—request really— that Alyssa Finchley come with me tonight? Max reversed the station wagon out of his parent's driveway and headed in the direction of the headland. Perversity, that's what it was. If he were honest with himself, it riled him to think that she considered him to be so unprofessional that he would slant his final report in favour of the developer. He had a point to prove and he wanted her to witness it.

Night had settled on the town, and he encountered little traffic on the darkened streets. Windows of houses were lit up, but a vast dark mass lay on the horizon, shimmering in places where the moonlight skimmed the water. He couldn't let Alyssa or anyone else question his conduct of this site investigation. Not only would his professional reputation in the region be at stake, but he needed the kudos of this job. Lucrative projects of this size didn't often come his way. He didn't begrudge a cent of it, but paying for Clara's treatment had not come cheaply. He'd had to mortgage the house.

He turned off the feeder road leading to the parking area by the headland and drove slowly over the pot-holed track. The headlights picked out shrubs on either side. When he pulled up and turned off the headlights, the dark closed around him like a thick blanket. He climbed out of the car and zipped up his jacket against the evening breeze, wishing he had thought to bring a hat. There was no sign of Alyssa. Perhaps she had changed her mind about coming. He took his backpack from the rear of the car and locked the vehicle behind him. He'd been silly to expect her to come.

"I'm here."

Max swung around to see Alyssa's shadowy figure silhouetted against the night sky, with the clifftop behind her and strands of hair blowing across her face. His first impression was of some mystical fantasy figure, with the moonlight shimmering on the sea behind her. She must have been sitting somewhere in the dark. Not many women would do that, walking through an area of remote scrub at night by themselves.

"Alyssa, that's you?"

She laughed at the absurdity of the question, and stepped closer. When he could see her more clearly, she looked totally normal. She was dressed sensibly in jeans and jacket, and with sneakers on her feet. She wore a beanie with a ridiculous pompom on the top, but strands of hair escaped from underneath it. With her hands jammed in her pockets, she looked ready for action.

Max cleared his throat, and reached into his backpack for the two headlamps, holding one out to Alyssa. "Put this on. It helps to keep your hands free. This shouldn't take us too long. Thanks for coming, by the way."

She shrugged, indicating it was of no consequence. Maybe not to her, but to him it was. He let her lead the way to the first installation. He could have found it on his own, but she knew her way around the site and strode confidently ahead. Following behind her gave him the opportunity of admiring her tush in a pair of well-fitting jeans. He was glad she couldn't see what he was looking at. She appeared to be comfortable in her body, lithely springing over rocks in their path before turning and grinning at him, as though to say, *Hey, can you keep up?*

The camera set-up at the first site hadn't been disturbed, and from what he could see, was fully operational. Same for the installations at each of the other locations. They kept conversation to a minimum, mindful of not broadcasting their presence too loudly. They didn't see any nocturnal activity, but that didn't mean no animals were there.

Back at the car, Alyssa handed him her headlamp. "I'm disappointed. I hoped we'd see some indication of nocturnal activity."

"We would have been very lucky. If there's anything to see, it should show up on the cameras, but it may take several nights before we see anything. They'll all be in hiding now."

He had no reason to hang around but found himself making small talk. Leaving Alyssa alone on the headland didn't seem right either, even though Seaclusion was only a short distance away.

"Thanks for coming down this evening. I realise this is just a passing interest for you; when your contract finishes, you'll head back to the city to get on with your life. Sandy Bay will be too quiet for you."

She shook her head. "Not a chance. I'm selling my property in the city. I've wiped the slate clean. There is no-one, correction, nothing to draw me back."

That did surprise him. Getting back into the city market would be difficult if she ever wanted to do that. His gut told him there was more to the story, but his head told him it was none of his business.

'You're obviously quite at home down here, even at night. I couldn't see you when I first pulled up."

"You weren't meant to, nor was anyone else. I was sitting on my rock, overlooking the ocean. From there, I can see the beach below, or anyone who approaches from the land. I'll show you if you have time."

He didn't have to rush home to Jeremy. "Sure. You've made me curious."

Alyssa led the way over a narrow path towards the cliff face. Before they reached the edge, the path opened out into a small clearing, central to which was a large flat-topped sandstone rock. Due to a bend in the coastline, they couldn't see all the lights of Sandy Bay but they could see Port Reilly in the distance. They could have been miles away from civilization. Max followed Alyssa's lead and perched himself on the rock beside her. The scene was incredibly peaceful. He hadn't had moments like this for such a long time. A pang of sadness made him aware of a huge hole in his life.

Their mood was more relaxed than on previous occasions. Perhaps they had reached a milestone in mutual trust. He hoped so.

"I can see why you like it. The view is spectacular."

"Mm… some nights you can't see much, but on a night like tonight when there's plenty of moonlight, it's almost magical. Sitting here replenishes my soul."

Alyssa lifted her face to the sky and shut her eyes. Wispy bits of hair that had escaped her beanie played around her face. Bathed in moonlight, her face looked inviting. Before he acknowledged to himself what he was doing, Max leaned forward and lightly brushed her lips with his. Her eyes sprang open. He read the astonishment reflected in the eyes just inches from his.

Oh shit… I shouldn't have done that.

His gut clenched as he waited for her to chew him out. She was a lawyer, for fucks sake. Next thing, he'd be up on a charge of sexual assault. He barely had time to register this thought before Alyssa wound an arm around his neck, and drawing his head down to hers, kissed him. The warmth of those pillowed, exploring lips stirred feelings that had been dormant for longer than he cared to acknowledge. He lost himself in the delicious sensation. This wasn't what he had expected, but then what had he expected? A simple and professional interaction.

Suddenly she jerked back, pushing against his chest with her hands before springing off the rock. "Sorry, please pretend that never happened."

Max stood up also, dusting the sandy grit from the seat of his pants. The moonlight created dancing patterns on the surging waves, and to his mind the scene laughed at him. "I can't pretend that. It did, and I'm not sorry, but I shouldn't have started it. Put it down to the location and a magical night. Perhaps this rock has special aphrodisiac properties."

She grimaced, brushing the hair from her eyes, and avoiding his. "I doubt it, but as an excuse it will have to do. I promise it won't happen again."

He was sorry to hear that, but she was right. He needed to focus on the job at hand, and tangling with Alyssa was an unnecessary complication. The lapping of the waves on the beach below underscored the uncomfortable silence.

"I think we've finished—"

"I'd better go—"

They began speaking at the same time, then stopped. Alyssa finally looked at him again, chewing at her lips before she spoke again. "I don't usually kiss my clients. Not even in the big city."

"Ex-client. The will is finalized, so we don't need to worry about that anymore. I promise I won't accost you again. Do you want a lift back to Seaclusion?"

"No thanks. It's not far, and I need the walk."

That didn't surprise him. He could have done with a walk in the night air to cool off as well. He led the way back to his car, and stood uncertainly by the driver's side door. "If you're still interested, I can let you know if anything shows up on the cameras."

"Absolutely. I didn't come out here tonight just for the hell of it. I'm genuinely interested in the results."

Her answer provided some relief to the tension that had built between them. "Great… well I mean, these results will be important in finalizing my report."

He smiled at her, and as though anticipating he might lean forward and kiss her again, Alyssa took a step back. "I'll see you then. Let me know what you find."

She turned abruptly and walked briskly back along the access road and towards the path that climbed the slope to where Seaclusion sat. He watched briefly, reassuring himself that she was safe, and then slipped behind the wheel and cruised slowly back to the public road and the route home. The evening had not turned out as he had expected. He wasn't sorry though, no matter what he'd said. He wasn't sorry at all.

9 – The Warning

A HEAVY WEIGHT sat on her chest. Alyssa took a breath and tried to roll over, confused as dream morphed into reality. Tiger kneaded her upper body with his front paws, purring loudly.

"Go away, cat. Let me sleep." Alyssa stretched under the blankets, relishing the warmth of the bed. She could happily go back to sleep. The cat resisted her attempts to dislodge him and resumed his kneading. She opened her eyes fully and noted the time on the bedside clock. Seven thirty.

"Shit!" She threw back the blankets, and jumped out of bed, unseating the cat off in the process. "Tiger, why didn't you wake me earlier?"

Breakfast consisted of a quick slice of toast with a smear of Vegemite, eaten as she slopped food into Tiger's bowl and stuffed her laptop back in its bag. She hardly ever slept so late. It wasn't as if the previous evening had been that taxing. Surprising maybe, but not unusually late.

Most of the morning traffic travelled against her as she drove the road between Sandy Bay and Port Reilly. Some people made a daily commute to the city. Crazy. Why would anyone want to do that? It looked like being a pleasant day locally, much better than battling city traffic.

Paul nodded a greeting when mug in hand, she wandered into the office kitchen in search of her morning coffee. He busied himself with topping up the machine with ground coffee. She liked that about the office: everyone pitched in with the mundane tasks. He wiped the benchtop where he had spilt some of the coffee.

"How was your weekend? You had a good crowd at the development site on Saturday."

"Thanks to Delia and the community team who broadcast news of the event, the attendance was gratifying. I can only hope that the people who needed to take note of our views on the project did so."

"I doubt it'll be that easy, but it's a start. I meant to ask; were there any problems with that file I passed to you for Max Saunders?"

No guesses why he'd segued into asking about Max. The project on the headland and Max were synonymous. "It was straightforward. He has executed the document, so it's taken care of."

"Good. I've nagged him for a while to get that finalised. I'm glad opposition to the development didn't get in the way of our professionalism."

Paul pressed the buttons that had the machine filling his mug. Alyssa had the uncomfortable feeling that Paul's comments were a thinly veiled message for her. Don't let your passion cause disruption for my business. Fair enough. She liked to think she was professional enough to rise above any pettiness. What would Paul say if he knew how the previous night had evolved? The question was irrelevant, as she would never tell him.

"I've left another file on your desk," he said, pausing at the kitchen door. "It's a succession document for a local family business. There are a few siblings involved and it's important we get this right. I've drafted it, but I'd appreciate your input."

"Sure. I'll get right onto it." Alyssa carried her coffee back to her office, making a mental note to water the pot plants later. Before that, she wanted to call Delia. She opened her laptop and organised her desk space before picking up her phone.

"Hi, Delia? Thanks so much for your input on Saturday. Your talk generated a lot of interest and helped to emphasize the importance of maintaining areas of natural vegetation."

"My pleasure. I sold a few copies of my book as well, so that was a win for me."

"Well deserved. Are you free to catch up for lunch this week? My shout. There's a great café overlooking the bay, The Saucy Fish, but you probably know it."

"I know it, but I've never eaten there. I'd love to join you. Wednesday would be a good day for me."

The week evolved into a range of deadlines. So much for a quiet life away from the city. Being busy meant not so much time to think, and that suited Alyssa just fine. A phone call to the real estate agent in Adelaide was on her to-do list, but she didn't complete the items above it. She rationalised if he had something to tell her, then he would put through a call to her.

In particular, she didn't have time to think about Max and the events of the previous Sunday evening.

Alyssa arrived first at the Saucy Fish and secured a table on the deck, overlooking the water. She watched as Delia threaded her way between the tables. The other woman looked around uncertainly before her face split into a smile when she spotted Alyssa.

"I love the location, it's an inspired choice. Well done you."

"I've been looking forward to this. I've warned the office I'll be late back from lunch. This is the least I can do to express my appreciation for your role last Saturday. You reached a wider audience of local residents; plus, the talk you gave was so interesting."

"Have you had any feedback?"

"Some from locals who attended, but nothing from council representatives or those with the power to make decisions. The media reports were helpful. I'm hoping to generate more coverage in the city as well."

The waiter arrived to take their orders, and conversation segued into debating the merits of the various options. Delia chose grilled whiting, and Alyssa couldn't go past the salt and pepper squid. She knew the squid had probably been pulled up from the local jetty in the previous twenty-four hours.

Delia was curious about Alyssa's work in Adelaide, and their discussion ranged over her involvement with environmental law, and then Delia's experiences in seeking funding for the work she did with species under threat. They were at the coffee stage, when a woman paused by their table.

"Delia! I've been meaning to catch up with you. How long are you in town? I bought a copy of your book, by the way. It's a present for my father on his birthday next week."

"Lovely to see you too, Emma. I'll be here for a couple of days yet. Alyssa has been very helpful in publicising the launch of the book in the local community."

Living in a small town meant interruptions were to be expected while out and about. Emma glanced at Alyssa, but her attention was focussed on Delia. Her white jeans fitted her snugly, and she'd teamed them with a white skivvy and pale pink vest, sold from a local store. Alyssa recognised it from a shop window display. Her blond hair fell just below her shoulders, and had the appearance of being casually styled, but curling tongs probably contributed to that.

Emma pulled out a chair and sat down. Delia cast an uncertain glance across the table. Alyssa was mildly irritated, but mentally shrugged. She could hardly tell the woman to piss off. "We're just having coffee. Would you like to join us?"

Emma beamed at Alyssa. "That would be lovely. Delia used to live next door to my family. Isn't it lucky I noticed you both."

"We've been discussing the book launch at the headland," Delia explained. "It coincided with the community meeting protesting against the resort development."

"It will probably still proceed, won't it?"

Alyssa tried not to roll her eyes. *Not if I've got anything to do with it.* "It's not a foregone conclusion, and will depend to some extent on the environmental assessment that's in progress."

Delia tilted her head enquiringly. "That would be the report being prepared by Max Saunders? He spoke to me on Saturday and purchased a copy of my book."

"Yes, he's still in the research phase. I accompanied him on Sunday when he set up motion sensor cameras to record any wildlife activity, and then went back that evening to check the installations were operational."

"You! But you're trying to stop the project. If Max wanted help from someone he can trust, he should have asked me."

Alyssa bristled at the suggestion she wan untrustworthy. "I think Max was keen to demonstrate his methodology to me. He seemed to think that having a lawyer vouch for the process was a good move, and I was keen to observe it."

Emma looked out over the water briefly before speaking again. "I'm always available to assist Max." Her tone was clipped and precise.

"Do you work in his business?"

"No, but we're very close. I promised Clara I would be there for Max and Jeremy. We were always good friends, but our relationship has deepened in the last two years. I could never replace Clara, but I've become a second mother to Jeremy. He's such a sweet child."

Alyssa thought back to the morning she drove back to Adelaide, when she saw Max sitting at the café with a woman. She recognised Emma now as that woman. She closed her eyes briefly in mortification. She'd made a total fool of herself.

"We're not rushing things", Emma continued. "It's not so long since Clara died, and I want Max to be very sure, but he's still young. It's not fair on him to be alone forever. Clara would never have wanted that."

Emma sipped her coffee, eyeing Alyssa over the rim of her cup. She didn't need to say anything else. The message was loud and clear. Max is mine; hands off. Lucky Alyssa wasn't looking for another man in her life. When she finished her coffee, she left the two other women to catch up on their shared history, paying the bill on her way out, including for Emma's coffee. She was welcome to it, and to Max as well for that matter.

Back in the office, Alyssa remembered she still hadn't rung Mark Pedlar. Phillip had a week before vacating the townhouse, but Mark had said he would canvas the potential purchasers on his database for pre-sale interest. He also said he would provide her with a market update.

Jodie had papered her desk with several post-it messages in her absence, and that, combined with the long lunch hour, meant that personal phone calls would have to wait. She made a mental note to call in the morning instead, moving it to the top of her to-do list. As it was, she didn't leave the office until nearly six thirty, and only then because Paul prompted her.

"You're not in the city now, you know. You're allowed to go home."

"What about you?"

"Guilty as charged. I'm on my way and you should be too."

Getting into her car, Alyssa was pleased the drive home was short. The pressures of the day had caught up with her. She wound down the windows of the car and tuned the radio to the local FM radio station. *Bohemian Rhapsody* filled the car and probably a portion of the coast road as well.

By the time she pulled up in the driveway, she had managed to switch off from work, but not her thoughts about Max. She'd accosted him, but he wasn't blameless. He'd made the first move. Where were his ethical standards if he had an understanding with Emma? He'd kissed another woman, and with passion as well. Perhaps the setting—moonlight, magical rock, heat of the moment carried him away, but was that an excuse? Maybe this was standard behaviour for all men.

She kicked off her shoes when inside and poured herself a glass of chilled Chablis. Sunset colours streaked the sky, and she wandered out onto the deck to make the most of the dwindling light. A calm had settled over the landscape and perhaps on her mood as well. She traced the outline of her lips with a finger, recalling the sensation of Max's mouth on hers. For that moment, it had been possible to forget where they were, and the fact that she'd sworn off men. Maybe she should wind a cord around her wrist as a reminder.

A soft meow in the vicinity of her feet reminded her she wasn't alone. Tiger brushed against her ankle, then looked up beseechingly, expecting either a head rub or some food. Probably both.

"Haven't forgotten you, Tiger. At least you're faithful to me, unless you've been cadging food and cuddles from the people next door."

The cat purred, and rising on hind legs, rubbed his head against her knee before dropping back on all fours. He might as well have said, "Of course I love you, but a cat never kisses and tells."

She had just finished washing the dishes from the quick stir-fry she'd prepared for her evening meal, when her phone rang.

"Alyssa, it's me… Phillip."

Once that voice would have made her heart sing. "What do you want?"

"I need to talk to you…" He paused and she heard him sigh. "Your real estate agent came around today to take some photographs. Alyssa, do you really have to sell the house? We were so good together; we could be again. I could come and stay for a few days while we talk it out."

"What happened to the girlfriend? Moved on already?"

"She could never compete with you. If you hadn't been so wrapped up in your work, I wouldn't have looked twice at her."

"So, it's all my fault then?"

"Of course not, that's not what I'm saying. It's just that… I missed you. You were so busy, and even when you were home, you brought files with you. I was never number one priority in your life."

"*We* were my priority. We were going to get married. Surely that's a major commitment on my part. You didn't see me cheating on you with some tart from the office."

"You were already married… to the job."

Silence hung heavily on the conversation. She couldn't deny what he said. She had immersed herself in her work, but that's what being a lawyer in the corporate world was all about. He knew that. It was also the job that helped to finance their lifestyle. He never complained about the perks.

"You could have talked to me about it instead of chasing someone else. What's happened? Has she thrown you over for someone more her own age?"

"Don't be so bitchy. It doesn't suit you."

"Maybe not, but bitchy is how I feel. I had such dreams for us, Phillip. I thought we'd have a family in that house. We'd talked about kids' names for chrissake. You destroyed that dream. I won't change my mind. I'm selling."

"Bitch."

Phillip disconnected the call, leaving her sitting and wondering. Had she been hasty and unreasonable? Not so long ago, she was convinced her future lay with Phillip. Perhaps is still did. It wasn't as if there was a romantic future for her in Sandy Bay. Staring at the phone as though it could yield answers, she resolved to sleep on it overnight. The morning might bring a new understanding.

Each time he returned to check the cameras, Max looked up at Oceanview. He half expected Alyssa to come tearing down the slope to slap him with an assault charge. She might think he'd lured her to the headland to accost her. On the other hand, she had invited him to see her special vantage point over the coast, and she had responded to his tentative approach Perhaps *she* was the one doing the luring.

In spite of the urging of Clara's parents, he wasn't in a hurry to re-partner. He had Jeremy to think of; the kid needed stability in his life, not more upheaval. Dating rules had probably changed since he and Clara first met. He would keep to himself—safer that way.

The stirrings of passion were unexpected. The closeness of her body, the roundness of her breasts as they rose and fell, the inviting lips as she tilted her head back in silent offering to the heavens… Was it any surprise he reacted as he did? She'd been more temptress than the Sirens of mythical Greece. In that fleeting moment, she had been impossible to resist. He wouldn't let it happen again.

10 – The Picnic

SLEEPING ON IT had seemed a good idea, but in the morning, Alyssa had no greater clarity about the decisions confronting her. Sell the house or not? Give Phillip a second chance or not?

"What do you reckon, Tiger? Surely, you've got sound advice?"

The cat stalked to his bowl and sat expectantly. The look he gave her indicated that the only question worth answering related to the delivery of his breakfast. She needed to speak to someone with better access to inside information. Charlotte. She might know whether the skank was still with Phillip, and any other relevant gossip.

She waited until seated at her desk with her morning cuppa before making the call.

"Hi there, girlfriend. How's coastal living treating you? I'll come and see you soon, I promise." Charlotte was disgustingly chirpy for so early in the day.

"Coastal living's treating me just fine. This is a quick call—I'm more interested in aspects of city living at the moment. Phillip rang me last night and asked me not to sell the house, and I was awake half the night wondering if I was being too hasty. He wants me to give him a second chance."

"You're not seriously considering taking him back, are you? Salt air must have addled your brain."

"That's always a possibility. I got the impression the skank had moved on. It might have been a rude awakening for him."

Charlotte gave a muted groan. "Listen to me. I'll even say it slowly so there are no mis-understandings. One, Phillip is the fella who couldn't keep it in his pants. Two, the young lady must have seen him for what he was. Three—this is probably what prompted the call—he's been turned down for a partnership with *Clegg and Drummond*, because questions were raised about his moral integrity."

"He didn't mention that to me! How do you know this?"

"I keep my ear to the ground. Clegg and Drummond are a conservative firm. My guess is that Phillip hopes that if you clasp him to your bosom again, his respectability rating will improve."

In response to the news, Alyssa stood and paced the room with the phone clutched to her ear. "I didn't realize that news of our breakup had spread, although one of the senior partners and I attended the same book club. She probably heard the news there, loyalty to the sisterhood, and all that."

"And rightly so. I can't tell you what to do, but Alyssa? You deserve better."

Alyssa digested this news in a moment's silence before giving a heartfelt sigh. "His betrayal hurts all over again. I must have been crazy to even contemplate taking him back.

He wasn't exactly sweet-talking me when he rang. Keep me posted, will you? You're a good friend."

She couldn't settle after disconnecting the call. She fetched water for her plants, and then stood at the window, watching the activity outside. People went about their business. Mothers pushed toddlers in strollers, couples sat at coffee tables, and cars drove past in an orderly procession. Life was so normal for all those people. Why couldn't it be so for her? She saw a woman sitting by herself at one of the tables, reading her tablet and drinking a coffee. The image was reassuring. Other people functioned happily on their own, and so would she.

Alyssa threw herself into work for the remainder of the week. It helped to take her mind off things, and Tiger smooched affectionately when she arrived home in the evenings. That helped as well. She told herself that life was for living; put on your big girl pants and get on with it.

With this resolution in mind, she took herself to the farmer's market on Saturday morning, and stocked up with seasonal produce, local cheese and olives, and a Chicken and Leek pie, earmarked for dinner. By now, she knew a few of the locals, and meet and greets took up most of the morning, before she dragged her purchases home and unpacked.

Goldilocks would have been pleased with the day. Not too hot and not too cold. Just right. She took a ploughman's lunch and a glass of local ginger beer out onto the deck with a book she'd found in Mary's bookcase and plonked herself in one of the outdoor chairs. A small piping voice broke through her concentration. She ignored it for a while, before registering that the sound was carrying up from the headland.

Drink in hand, she wandered over to the deck railing and looked down. A car had parked off the road, and two people, one big and one small stood beside it. The small person looked up and waved enthusiastically. Jeremy. She saw Max unload some bags and a blanket from the back of the car. They were having a picnic. Max looked at Jeremy and then up at her, giving her a small nod of acknowledgement.

Not as enthusiastic as your son. Alyssa waved in response, before moving back to her chair and sitting again. She hadn't seen Max since the previous Sunday night. A flush of embarrassment swept over her as she remembered the kiss, as she'd thought of it through the week; a spontaneous and passionate kiss. She wasn't going to apologise, especially since he'd started it, but if she didn't speak to him now, she would feel increasingly awkward. She couldn't avoid him in a town the size of Sandy Bay, and they were mutual friends of Paul and Jacinta.

One of her purchases that morning had been a lamington cake, intending to take it to work for morning tea on Monday. The cake could be put to a better use. She cut off several slices and put them into a plastic container. She packed the basket with the cake, a fresh bottle of ginger beer and three glasses. She also grabbed a pair of binoculars, knowing they might be useful.

Checking first that Max and Jeremy were still below, she set off down the hill, clutching her basket. The car was there, but she couldn't see them. She knew where they would be; the secret picnic place. Even if she didn't know, Jeremy's excited chatter would have led her there. She pulled aside the foliage growing over the path and stepped into the clearing.

"Is this a private party, or can anyone join in?" She focused on Jeremy rather than Max.

"Hey, Alyssa. Dad and I are having a picnic in the secret place you showed us."

"It's about time another kid had a good time here. All sorts of adventures happen here."

"You're not wrong about that."

Glancing sideways, she noticed that Max wasn't looking at her, but she knew the words spoken under his breath were for her benefit.

"I brought some more picnic food in case you didn't have enough." She placed the basket on the blanket which had been spread out on the ground, and addressed Max directly. "Any news from the camera traps?" That was a safe opening gambit.

"Yes and no. There have been a few small lizards, and a fox one night and a cat on another. Those last two combined would probably ensure that no local marsupials are going to be found but unless I looked, I had no way of knowing for sure."

"That's disappointing. I hoped that something interesting would show up."

"I've left the cameras in position for now. Sometimes these things take a while. For now, I'm working on the assumption that there are no native marsupials in the area."

"What's this?" Jeremy asked, having spotted the binoculars in her basket.

"They help you to look at things that are far away and to see them clearly. We used to look through them we had our picnics down here. I'll show you."

She led him to a vantage point where he could see parts of the town and showed him how to adjust the focus. With the child now entranced with what he could see, she turned back to his father.

"Max, I think an apology is in order. I didn't—"

"Sure. I should have called you through the week. I'm sorry for making a pass. It was grossly inappropriate."

Not entirely, but I'm not telling you that. "No, I meant to apologise. God, that's all I seem to do these days, where you're concerned at least. I shouldn't have reacted as I did, especially given your other commitments."

He frowned as though confused. "I wasn't expecting you to apologise to me. I promise it won't happen again. Can we put it down to an unreal setting, effect of moonlight and a sudden mental aberration?"

Alyssa hadn't paid attention to the well-modulated tone to his voice before. It spoke to her of a cross between smooth chocolatey notes with an underlying huskiness that was oddly appealing. The green eyes regarding her earnestly caused the teeniest catch in her breath.

She took a quick breath to quell the sensation and smiled at him in relief. "I haven't been considered a mental aberration before, but I think we can safely put the incident aside and move on. It doesn't mean I'm not still opposed to the project. I haven't changed my mind about that."

"I would have been surprised if it did." He reached out as though to place a hand on her shoulder, then paused with an odd look crossing his face and dropped his hand to his side and he turned his attention to his son.

"Jeremy, don't drop those binoculars. Are you hungry? We should have something to eat. That's what picnics are all about."

The suggestion of food brought the boy scuttling back to them. He thrust the binoculars back at Alyssa. "These are great. I'll ask my dad to buy me some. Max gave her a look that clearly said, *Now look what you've done.*

"We've got some at home. I didn't think to bring them today. I'm a novice at this picnic business. Are you joining us on the rug?" The question was directed to Alyssa.

"Of course. I've had lunch up on the deck, but some cake never goes astray."

As they sat on the rug, Jeremy gave them a running commentary on the sorts of animals that might live on the headland, ranging from tigers to wolves and indicating a vivid imagination. He looked over his shoulder occasionally, as though expecting a wild beast to break through the shrubs. Fortunately for them all, none did.

"Did you know I'm a fast runner?" he asked Alyssa. "We've got sports day at school next week and I'm going to be running in two of the races."

"Good luck for that. I'm sure you'll run as fast as one of those wolves. Pretend there's a tiger chasing you, and you'll run even faster."

He giggled before turning to his father. "You're going to watch, aren't you, Dad."

"Sure. What day is it again?"

"Wednesday. I brought a note home from school about it. After the races, we get to go home early."

Max's face dropped. "I've got a meeting in the city on Wednesday, mate. I can't get out of this one. I'll see if Grandpa can go in my place. He would like to do that, I'm sure."

Jeremy's face crumpled. "But I want you to watch."

"I know, and I'm really sorry, but I didn't have any say about the timing of this meeting. If I can get back early I will. Perhaps we can have pizza for tea."

Jeremy's bottom lip dropped. He didn't look convinced, in spite of the proposed treat. Father and son stared at each other. Alyssa cleared her throat. "This is only a suggestion and don't feel you need to take notice of it, but I could go, if I sort out my work calendar for that afternoon. I'm reasonably sure I don't have any specific commitments."

Max turned to her in surprise and Jeremy also with obvious delight.

"Are you sure about this?"

"Would you really watch me run? Yay!"

"I'd love to," she said, mentally crossing her fingers. School sports days were way out of her comfort zone. She had probably skived off during her school days, never having been the sporty type "Tell me when and where, and I'll be there. The office works on a flexible basis and I'm sure Paul will be supportive when he knows who's involved."

"Well, if you're sure it's not too much trouble…"

"It's not, but I don't want to tread on anyone's toes. If Grandpa prefers to go, I quite understand, or anyone else…?"

Surely this is something Emma would attend, given how close she said they were. Strange that Max hasn't mentioned her.

"But I want you to go." Jeremy spoke emphatically.

Max shrugged in resignation. "I'll text you the details. Actually, I don't have your mobile number. He pulled his phone from his pocket and after swiping to unlock the screen, looked at her expectantly. Alyssa dictated her number and recorded his in her phone also. She had his contact details on file at work, but when there was a child involved, she should be able to contact him easily.

"That's decided then. I'll leave you both to finish your picnic. See you on sport's day, Jeremy."

As she climbed back up the path to Seaclusion Cottage, she could hear Jeremy's excited voice behind her. She hoped she wouldn't come to regret this decision.

***

The last thing he had expected was Alyssa to offer to attend the sports day. She didn't come across as someone who was child orientated. If he had to summarise her, it would be more career-focused, professional, conscientious. That didn't involve keeping company with small boys who were sometimes boisterous, smelly, whined and if you were lucky, demonstrated all three attributes at once.

He glanced up at her retreating figure. Perhaps he'd missed out a bit. Surprisingly passionate, but he needed to put that thought out of his mind. She could change from focused and engaged to lighting up with laughter in the blink of an eye. He was never sure which version he would encounter. Unpredictable; that probably described her best.

Under different circumstances, he might have asked Emma to attend the sports day, but that could make life more complicated than he wanted. Sometimes, Emma made assumptions and he didn't need that headache, nor the issue messing with Jeremy's head. Aunty Emma should stay that way.

The temperature began to cool. He looked around their picnic haven. He could imagine the kids having a fantastic time in the past, particularly in the days when children had the luxury of being free-range kids. People had larger families then, and there was safety in numbers. Not like the sole parent families that were the norm now. If things had been different, he and Clara might have had more children, but that had not been an option as her health declined.

Alyssa's opposition to the project was understandable. Dammit, he didn't want it to go ahead either. It should be preserved for future generations. The proposed development should happen elsewhere. Still, being commissioned to undertake the environmental study had been good for his bottom line. He folded up the blanket, while Jeremy watched.

"Dad… it will be good if Alyssa can watch me run, won't it?"

"Sure will, mate. Time to pack up; we need to be getting home."

"Can I look through your binoculars?"

"Sure. When we get home. Carry the blanket, we're out of here."

As he stashed the blanket and the remainder of their picnic gear in the car, he hoped he was headed for a low-stress week. The meeting in town was to give a preliminary report on his findings and he knew he would be under pressure to wrap the work up, and to be supportive of the proposal. Professional integrity meant standing his ground. Dammit. If only the cameras had captured the result he'd been hoping for.

11 – Race Day

"WHAT MADE ME promise something like that? I know nothing about sport and even less about kids."

Tiger clearly didn't care one way or the other. He gave her a disdainful look and stalked off to find a sunny area of the deck. It had been a spur of the moment decision to make the offer the preceding day, and she would have to make the most of it. If she found out what time Jeremy's race was scheduled, she wouldn't have to stay very long. She could always review files on her laptop if she had too long to wait. Alyssa made a mental note to put a fold-up chair in the car and to take a hat.

She found her own sunny location on the deck, seated at the outdoor table. She had somewhere to park her coffee and could scroll through the morning's news. The conversation with Philip still preyed on her mind. She couldn't decide what upset her more; the abuse he delivered, or the fact he was trying to use her and their relationship to save his career. In spite of that, she was sorry he'd been turned down by

Drummond and Gregg. She knew how much he had wanted that promotion.

Had he ever loved her, or was their relationship merely a convenience? She thought back over their years together. There were tender times and they had seemed to be genuine. She would try to hold onto those memories and shut out his recent behaviour.

Watching the real estate market had become compulsive. She scrolled through the online listings in the suburb in which her townhouse was located, searching for comparable sales, and then began scrolling through listings in other areas as she debated where she might live instead. Until she knew how much cash she had to play with, the search was purely theoretical. Anything she really liked seemed to be way over her budget. At least she didn't have to make an immediate decision. The townhouse had been purchased with the vague idea that one day it would be a family home, but now she could please herself, and only consider her needs.

She broke the news to Paul about attending the sports day over their customary coffee in the kitchen the next morning before getting stuck into the week.

"You're doing what? I didn't think you two were that friendly."

"We're not… I mean, we're not unfriendly… it's for Jeremy really. He was so sad that nobody would watch his race, so I volunteered."

"Doesn't Jeremy have grandparents who would probably love to watch their grandson run?"

Alyssa rolled her eyes. She knew Paul was trying to get a rise out of her. "I believe he has grandparents and probably they would love to watch him run. The thing is, I promised him I would go seeing as his father couldn't, so I have to." She huffed at him. "You did tell me this was a flexible working environment, within reason. Surely this is *within reason* unless something of major importance crops up in the meantime?"

He grinned. "Sure. Just wait until I tell Jacinta."

"Paul! There is absolutely nothing to tell."

"No, of course not."

He smirked as he left the kitchen, and Alyssa had to restrain herself from throwing the dish brush at him. She didn't need infuriating insinuations first thing on a Monday morning.

Max rang her on the Tuesday to check that she hadn't forgotten and still intended turning up.

"Of course, I'll go. I told Jeremy I will. Do you know what time his race is likely to start?"

"If you're there by one, you should be fine. It kicks off after lunch. Head on over to the school oval. Jeremy is in the Blue Team, so if you park yourself near the blue flags, you should be fine. I'll tell him to watch out for you."

"Sounds too easy. I'll be there."

"Thank you for this. I owe you one. Can you drop him off to his grandparents when the event is over, and I'll pick him up from there?"

The arrangements seemed straight forward. Max gave her the address of his in-laws and Alyssa assured him his son would be delivered there as soon as the children were discharged from school. She wondered again the following morning on the wisdom of making the offer, when a couple of work matters threatened to derail the day. Of all days to have unexpected deadlines, it had to be that day.

"Don't worry, I can handle it," Paul said. "Just focus on your day off. You've put in enough overtime, so you've earned this break. Enjoy!"

Enjoy! I'm not sure that's the right terminology for attending a school sports' day. Alyssa kept those thoughts to herself as she checked off the things she needed to take: sunglasses, hat, sunscreen, chair, laptop... *nope. That can stay behind. I won't be able to see the screen in the sunshine, anyway.*

The scene at the oval was overwhelming when she arrived. There were huddles of parents, teachers with clipboards and whistles, and lines of highly excitable children. She found the blue flags and some shade as well, where she could position her chair out of the sun. Jeremy saw her and waved enthusiastically. She saw him speak to a teacher briefly before racing over to greet her.

"You came! We've got a printed timetable to give to our mum and dad, but I haven't got a mum, not any more... just a dad. Should I give the paper to you?"

"Of course, I came. I said I would." She smiled brightly at the small boy. "If I could have a look at the list, that would be helpful. Then I'll know when your race is about to be run."

Jeremy's races were marked with a highlighter, and she saw that his individual race would take place in about half an hour, and he was participating in a relay shortly after that. She settled down in her chair, slapped her hat firmly on her head, and cheered when the blue team looked like they were doing well.

She knew some of the other parents by sight, and exchanged nods, but mostly they were in their own parent groups. One of the people she recognised was Emma, the woman she had met while lunching with Delia. She put her sunglasses on and slunk down in her seat. Alyssa had no interest in connecting with Emma, and surmised that the feeling was probably mutual. They hadn't exactly hit it off on that occasion.

When Jeremy's race was called, Alyssa stood up and moved down to the starting line. Parents were asked to keep clear, but she managed to catch his eye and give him a thumbs-up, mouthing *good luck* at him. He grinned at her briefly before getting ready to run, fists tightly clenched at his side and a serious expression on his face. For a while, he ran neck and neck with another child, but at the last minute, that little boy pulled ahead, and Jeremy came a close second. He looked crestfallen, but she gave him a high-five as he jogged back to his team group, still panting from his exertion.

"You're right. You run really fast Jeremy. You did well."

"But I didn't win."

"You were very close. Your dad will be pleased when we tell him."

Jeremy didn't appear totally convinced, but a few minutes later she saw that he was cheering for the next team race, seemingly having moved on. When time came for the relay race, he fared better. The blue team came in first, resulting in much jubilation, but from the children and the watching blue parents.

Alyssa glanced at her watch, wondering how much longer before the sports day finished. Perhaps she could take Jeremy to get an ice cream from the new shop in town before delivering him to his grandparents. It would probably be another half hour at least. Her phone beeped with incoming messages and in spite of her earlier resolution to leave work at the office, she settled back in her chair and scrolled through, looking for anything that needed urgent attention.

She sent off a couple of quick replies and was just slipping it back into her bag when the phone rang. A couple of parents looked around, frowning at the ringtone interruption. She glanced at the screen. Philip. What did he want now? Her finger hovered over the Reject Call button, but then curiosity got the better of her.

"Phillip? This is not a good time."

"It never is. I needed to—"

Another race had begun, and the level of shrieking from the watching kids reached an ear-splitting crescendo. Alyssa rose from her chair, clamped one hand over her other ear to block out the noise, and moved several meters away where she could hear him more clearly.

"It's noisy here. I didn't hear what you just said."

"I said I'm coming down… to Sandy Bay."

She stained to hear him over the nose. "What? Why?"

"To see you, of course. I need to speak to you in person. I've booked into the Regal Hotel on the Esplanade."

"When?" She walked a little further away and turned her back on the crowd in an effort to catch what he said. She wasn't sure she heard him correctly.

"I'll drive down on Friday evening. I've booked accommodation for the weekend."

"The last time you spoke to me, you called me a bitch. What's changed?"

"Babe, you know I get excitable sometimes, but it doesn't mean anything. It doesn't change what I feel for you."

This conversation was getting ridiculous. Alyssa squinted over her shoulder to where the activity was taking place. It all seemed a lot quieter now. "Phillip, I have to go. This is not a good idea. I'll speak to you later."

She didn't wait for his response, but disconnected the call. She walked back to her chair and looked around for Jeremy. Some of the parents were walking off with their children and it looked as though the school was packing up. Alyssa made her way to where she'd last seen him with his friends. A couple of boys still waited for their parents.

"Hey, have you kids seen where Jeremy Saunders went?"

They looked at her blankly and shrugged their shoulders. She scanned the crowd over their heads. Perhaps he'd gone to the toilet. Looking around, she spotted the toilet block fifty meters away. She set off in that direction, keeping an eye out for him as she went. She hovered outside when she arrived at the block. She couldn't go into the male toilets, but felt a bit strange lurking outside.

Eventually she managed to get the attention of a passing father and asked him to check for her. No Jeremy. He suggested she check with the teachers.

Of course. Why didn't I do that before?

She made her way back to where the teachers who supervised the blue team were still packing up and watching over those whose parents hadn't yet picked them up. She approached one of them.

"Excuse me, do you know where I would find Jeremy Saunders?"

"And you are…?"

"I'm a friend of his father's. I've been watching his races today and said I would drop him off at his grandparent's house when the events were over, but he seems to have disappeared."

The teacher regarded her with suspicion, her head tilted to one side. "That's odd. He just left with a woman who said she was his aunt."

Alyssa stared at her, aghast. "But he was supposed to leave with me. How could you let him go like that?"

The woman held up her hands defensively. "Don't get mad at me. I'm not his regular teacher. He referred to her as Aunt Emma and went off with her very happily."

Emma! I should have guessed."

Alyssa stared at the woman for a while, her thoughts whirring. She needed to make sure that Jeremy had been delivered to his grandparents as agreed, and then ring Max. She grabbed her camp chair and almost ran back to the car, with her anger increasing with every stop. How dare the woman snatch Jeremy like that?

She left rubber on the road on the drive to the grandparent's house. Her agitation increased significantly as she drove. Irresponsible. The woman was totally irresponsible. When she pulled up at the address, another vehicle was in the driveway. She heard voices inside the house as she approached the screen door, one of them being Jeremy's. He was giving a highly excited rendition of his team's performance in the relay. So he was there!

Alyssa rapped on the door. An elderly woman opened it with a polite but enquiring smile.

"Sorry to intrude. I was with Jeremy at the sport's day and he suddenly disappeared. I was told he left with an aunt, and wanted to check he was delivered safely here."

"You must be Alyssa. Max said you would be dropping him off. Thank you for checking, but yes, he's here. A family friend picked him up."

Emma appeared at the grandmother's shoulder. "You abandoned Jeremy and so I brought him home. I saw you ignoring him and on your phone. He's only a small boy. How could you have treated him like that?" She was full of self-righteous indignation.

Alyssa gaped at her. "That's an outrageous accusation. I took a quick phone call, but definitely did not abandon him."

"No harm done. He's here now and having some afternoon tea. Thank you for checking on him." Jeremy's grandmother took the conciliatory approach, looking quickly from Emma to Alyssa and clearly wanted to put a stop to any recriminations. "I'll tell Max you dropped by"

There was nothing further to be gained from the conversation and Alyssa nodded her thanks and stalked back to her car. She needed to call Max. She was reaching for her phone, still in the bottom of her bag, when it rang. She looked at the screen display. Max.

"Max! I was about to ring you."

"And tell me what? That you'd deserted my son?" The tone was cutting. No guesses as to who had already rung him.

"That's nonsense. I received a phone call during the last race. I moved away so that I could hear, and when I disconnected the call, Jeremy was gone. I looked everywhere for him."

"As I heard it, you sat there scrolling through your phone, totally disengaged with the event and ignoring Jeremy. Couldn't you leave work away for just a couple of hours? You offered to go… you didn't have to so why turn your back on him?"

Alyssa closed her eyes and counted to five before speaking again, enunciating slowly and clearly. "You've clearly been speaking to the woman who took it upon herself to drag him away while my back was turned. I don't know why you didn't ask her to attend in the first place, given that she's Jeremy's second mother."

"She's not… I didn't… it doesn't detract from the fact you ignored him." He paused, and then spoke in a tone devoid of emotion. "I trusted you with my son. If Emma wasn't there, anyone could have taken him."

"He's safe, your in-laws will attest to that. I'll leave you to your version of events."

She disconnected the call. The beginnings of a headache loomed and she rubbed at her temple. First Phillip, and now this. She needed to go home to some peace and quiet. She didn't need further grief from either of them.

***

He should have known Alyssa couldn't tear herself away from her work for long. He'd worked so hard to shield Jeremy from feelings of abandonment after his mother's death, and now Alyssa callously ignored him as well. Thank goodness Emma was there to step in and take over. Perhaps he should have asked her in the first place, although that entailed problems he didn't want to encourage.

He was angry with himself as much as with Alyssa. He'd allowed himself to enjoy her company and that was stupid. Why get tangled up with a woman who was only in town for a while, and had already stirred up trouble in the short time she'd been in the job. Jeremy liked her and that was another problem. He didn't want him to get attached to someone who wouldn't be sticking around. Best to avoid her in future.

He pulled up in front of Gordon and Rose's house, noting that Emma's car was still in the driveway. Only to be expected, he supposed. He'd only just stepped out of the car when Jeremy burst out of the house and ran to meet him.

"Dad… I came second and we won the relay. Alyssa said I ran really fast. She yelled loudly. I could hear her."

"She watched you?"

"Of course, she did. She waved and jumped up and down."

This version of events differed from the one Emma had given. "That's great, mate. I'm sorry I wasn't there to watch."

"Yeah, I know." Jeremy frowned. "Alyssa said we were going to get ice cream on the way home, but Emma said we couldn't wait for her. We had to go."

Max frowned. "But Alyssa had wandered off. You couldn't see her."

"No, she hadn't. She was on the phone, but not far away. I was going to wait by her chair, but Emma said you wanted me to go with her."

Did she now. Max had the feeling he'd been played for a fool. He heard the squeal of the screen door and looked over to where Emma stood in the doorway, smiling uncertainly in his direction. Wondering what Jeremy had told him, no doubt.

"I haven't forgotten it's pizza tonight. I'll say hello to Grandma and Grandad, and then we'll go."

He locked the car behind him, and headed towards the front door where Emma waited. This was a conversation he didn't want to have, and his stomach churned in anticipation.

"Hi Emma. Thank you for dropping Jeremy off."

"No problem. I couldn't leave him hanging around on his own. If you'd mentioned you weren't going to be there, I could have looked after him. As it turned out, I had to anyway."

"The thing is, Emma, he wasn't on his own. Alyssa was there and Jeremy knew where she was. By taking him away from the venue like that, without letting her know what you were doing, you caused her angst and worry. You could have waited with him until she had finished her call, or if really concerned, could have called me for advice."

Her face dropped. "I only wanted to help. I was worried for Jeremy, and I promised Clara I'd be there for him. I only wanted to honor my promise to her. You know how fond I am of him."

"Yes, I know, and he's fond of you too. Just..." He hesitated, wanting to find the right words. Don't smother us sounded a bit harsh. "... stick to our arrangements in future, and if there's any doubt, call me."

He exchanged greetings with his parents-in-law before shoveling Jeremy and his school things into the car. As he drove off, he was conscious of Emma's miserable face watching them. She had probably assumed she would get pizza with him and if the situation had been any different, he might have extended an invitation, but not today. There were now two women he wanted to avoid.

12 – The Visit

HER BURNING FACE felt hotter than the car seat on a summer's day. His attitude had seriously pissed her off. How dare he speak to her like that. As for Emma… that woman was a manipulative troublemaker. Alyssa stewed all the way home in the car.

More than anything, she felt stupid. She had begun to relax into a friendship with Max Saunders, but should have known that like most men, he had led her on. She had given more credence to their growing friendship than he had. Her initial reaction on receiving Phillip's phone call was to refuse to meet up with him, but after that conversation with Max, she might change her mind.

Perhaps she should rethink her current life plan, if you could call it that. Retreating from the city to Sandy Bay had seemed like a smart move, giving her time and space in which to emotionally regroup, but maybe she should have stayed in the city. Too bad, because she was committed to her current role until that contract terminated.

When she arrived back at Seaclusion Cottage, she kicked off her shoes and poured herself a glass of wine from the opened bottle in the fridge. Tiger came brushing around her legs.

"Tiger, go away. I've sworn off men, and as you're a bloke that has to mean you too."

The cat gave her a baleful look and maintained the pressure until she caved in and fed him. "I'll make an exception for you, although it's probably just cupboard love. You only hang around because I feed you."

She would have rung Charlotte to unload and debrief, but she hadn't mentioned Max before and certainly didn't want to mention Phillip's phone call. No prizes for guessing what her reaction would be to that news. She was still turning over her options when her phone rang. Not Phillip again?

"Hello?... Mary! So good to hear your voice."

"Why? Nothing's wrong, is it?"

"Not really. It's just been one of those days. I've met up with Delia a couple of times. She's pleasant company and did a great job at her book launch. She helped the cause immensely, and sold a few books as well, so that was a win-win."

"Anything else I should know about?"

Mary knew her too well. She always sensed when she was troubled. Alyssa sighed before answering. "You'd think I knew better at my age, but the short answer is *men.* The long answer is I've got on the wrong side of Max Saunders, thanks to the interference of a local woman called Emma, and Phillip rang earlier. He's coming down to Sandy Bay this weekend. He wants to talk."

"About what?"

"The house, us, the universe… perhaps all three. I'm not totally sure. He's staying at the Regal."

"Alyssa, you're a sensible woman. Phillip is looking after his own needs first, and you need to look after yours. If those needs coincide, that is a wonderful thing, but if they don't, you're strong enough to walk away. You can review your relationship more objectively now that you have put some distance between you."

"You're right. I just needed to be reminded of that fact."

"As for Emma… I know of her. Sandy Bay is like that. I'd suggest you keep out of her orbit, and you don't need dramas with Max any more than you need them with Phillip."

"You're right… as always. I'll stick to Tiger from now on. Enough about me… tell me your news."

The rest of the call passed in a brief update of her travels, which was the main reason for her call, that and to check that she and Tiger were fine. The detail would be communicated via email.

Paul greeted her in the office the next day. "How was the sport's day? I heard you misplaced young Jeremy Saunders." His words were lightly spoken but his expression was serious."

"Who said that? I did nothing of the kind. The child was abducted by a weird woman while my back was turned."

"Look… I don't want to tell you what to do, but Max is both a friend and a client of the practice. On a personal level, I don't want to see his life messed up any more than it already has been, and on a professional level, I don't want the practice brought into disrepute through mis-management of a client's affairs."

She stiffened. The temptation to put her coffee down on the bench, pick up her bag, and walk out the front door was strong. "If you have factual evidence of any wrong-doing on my part, I'll have no hesitation in handing in my resignation. I suggest that in this instance however, your informant did not have accurate information."

She didn't wait for his reply, but grabbed her coffee and stalked down the passage to her office, slopping some of the drink on the floor as she went. *Crap.* She would clean the mess up later. She needed to practice her deep-breathing exercises first. If a client weren't due in a few minutes, she would have taken a walk to clear her head. Not possible.

The conversation had one result though. Any hesitation she'd had about meeting up with Phillip was gone. She would listen to what he had to say and make her mind up from there. She didn't have to stay in Sandy Bay. Even her contract with Paul was not unbreakable. As Mary had said, she had to work out what was best for her. Mid-morning, her phone rang with Max's caller ID on the screen. She pressed reject.

Phillip was true to his word, and rang mid-evening on Friday to say he had arrived and had checked into his hotel.

"Fancy joining me for a nightcap?

"It's a bit late, isn't it?"

"You have settled into coastal life. You'd just be getting ready to go out in the city."

He was right. A lot of things had changed since she moved to Sandy Bay, social life being one of them. She was more inclined to settle down in a comfy chair with a good book and a mug of chocolate, or else catch up on a murder-mystery repeat on television. At this rate, she'd be classified as staid and boring.

"Okay, but not for long. It's been a challenging week. I'll meet you in the bar in thirty minutes."

Her stomach churned slightly at the thought of seeing Phillip again. She agonized over what to wear. It had to be something not too casual, but not over the top either. She would hate him to think she was making a special effort for him, but on the other hand, didn't want him to think she had let herself go. Her at-home style these days was more comfortable than chic.

In the end, she donned straight-leg black jeans, ankle boots, and a loose top of swirling blues and greens. She applied a light layer of make-up, but kept it simple. The lounge area attached to the bar was full of Friday night revelers when she walked in, but finding Phillip wasn't difficult. Besides his height, he stood out as someone from the city. His Hugo Boss suit, his hairstyle, polished shoes and heavy gold watch all proclaimed him to be a professional man of enviable status.

Alyssa's heart did a little jump when she spotted him. This was the man she'd been attracted to for so long, and a flood of conflicting emotions threatened overwhelm. He stood on her approach, and reaching out, kissed her on the cheek. She thought he was moving in for a kiss on the lips, and was about to turn her face away when he grazed her cheek instead. That was interesting. He smiled, a look that reminded her of the old Phillip.

"Hey babe, you look great. You've let your hair grow longer. I like it."

Alyssa patted her hair self-consciously. "I haven't looked around for a hairdresser yet. I keep meaning to ask for recommendations."

"You can always slip up to the city for an appointment with your old stylist. It's not that far. Enough about your hair… tell me what you've been doing in down-town Sandy Bay."

What *had* she been doing exactly? Nothing that would sound exciting to someone heavily involved in city-based corporate life. "Learning the ropes with Densley and Associates, then learning how to relax. Like you've indicated, my life revolved around work in the city; here I'm exploring some work-life balance. I'm trying to think of it as life-work balance."

He laughed. "I'm impressed. That's a big change. Maybe I should try it as well."

Alyssa inwardly stiffened. She'd expected that Phillip would launch into his spiel about why she shouldn't sell the house, and that she should come back to him and he hadn't said a word about that. He was playing his cards carefully.

"It's not all work. I'm also involved in a local community project. It's a David and Goliath issue really, but I'm rallying community support against a local development. Some of my legal experience may help with opposing a commercial development on land zoned for community use."

He chuckled "Sounds right up your alley. Take a seat while I get you a drink. Your usual?"

She nodded, and he headed in the direction of the bar while she selected a chair by the window, overlooking the bay. The jetty, lit by strategic lights, stretched out in the foreground.

She knew that families and the occasional lovers were probably strolling their way over the wooden planks to the far end, where the night fishermen would be guarding their lines. She had made that walk many times, but always with family, never with a lover.

She still ruminated on this fact when Phillip returned with her gin and tonic, took the seat opposite hers, and raised his glass in toast.

"I guess you're wondering what this weekend trip is all about. I want to reassure you that I didn't come down here to pressure you. I was an arse, and I acknowledge that. There may have been mitigating issues in our relationship, but I'm a grown man and made my own choices."

"Well, if it's not a rude question, why did you come down?"

Phillip looked out the window, appearing to gather his thoughts. "We haven't had closure. Letting our relationship disintegrate like it did, ignored all the good times we had together, and there were many." His eyes now met hers. "The term *conscious uncoupling* is a bit twee, but I think we both deserve better than acrimony."

Alyssa sat in stunned silence. She hadn't expected this. She hadn't forgotten Charlotte's revelations, but this… after their earlier conversations and the accusations thrown around, she hadn't expected such a turn-around. A little voice inside said, *Hey girl, don't be taken in. You know Phillip's a skilled negotiator. He's very good at his job.*

On the other hand, there was truth in what he said. To simply write off the years they had spent together was to deny an important part of her life. They each deserved more than that. She had to fight the tears and the lump in her throat that threatened to destroy the moment.

"It wasn't the ending I envisaged," she finally admitted, sipping her drink and relishing the bitter explosion as the liquid slid down her throat. "You didn't have to come all this way to tell me that."

"Yes, I did. Some things are best said in person, don't you think?"

She had no argument with that statement. It was the best way to ensure closure. The evening passed easily with general conversation, talking about acquaintances and catching up on news. Alyssa remained wary on the inside for all that, waiting for him to drop the hard word. He didn't. After two drinks, she glanced at her watch. "I don't keep the same hours that I did in the city. It's time I headed back to Seaclusion. What are your plans for the remainder of your visit?"

"That depends on you, to an extent. Besides the inevitable walk along the beach, I thought we could do dinner tomorrow evening."

"I'll let you know about that." She wasn't ready to commit to too much. She wanted time to digest this version of Phillip. Breakfast could be an easier option. "There's a farmer's market in the morning. You might like to meet up there for breakfast as a change from the hotel buffet."

"That sounds a better option. Tell me when and where, and I'll see you there."

She gave him directions and confirmed a meeting location before taking her leave. He walked her to her car, and again only bussed her on the cheek. It was like the parting of two old friends. Bemused thoughts crowded her head on the drive home. The weekend would be an interesting adjunct to her shitty week.

❧

Phillip waited at the designated meeting point when Alyssa parked her car and walked to meet him. The market already bustled, and they were greeted by the sight of fruit and vegetables laid out in pyramids, cartons of eggs, jars of honey, and freshly baked bread and pastry goods. The smell passing the bread stall was tantalizing, and left Phillip asking plaintively where they were going to eat. Alyssa made him wait until she had completed a few purchases.

"If I don't get these things now. They'll be sold out when I come back. It won't take long."

She'd brought a canvas tote with her, and filled it with an assortment of fruit and vegetables, plus her favourite cheese and a loaf of kalamata sour dough.

"That's all I need. We can get breakfast at the Juniper Café at the other end of the market. They have good coffee and a reliable menu."

"Sounds good to me. I'd eat anything right now. Let me carry that bag. We'll get there quicker that way."

Alyssa smirked at the histrionics, but gladly handed over the bag and led the way to the café. The tables inside were taken, but there were still a couple available on the veranda. They grabbed one, and Phillip lowered the bag to the ground at Alyssa's feet.

"You mind the table while I go inside to get the menus and I'll order our coffees to start with. I assume you'll have your usual?"

"Yes. That would be lovely… thank you."

He hurried into the café. She was amused at his insistence of remembering her preferences, almost as though he were trying to remind her of how well he knew her.

"Alyssa! I've been trying to call you."

No guesses as to who was behind her. Alyssa swiveled in her chair. Max and Jeremy stood there, evidently on their way to the market stalls.

Max stepped closer. "I need to apologise. I jumped the gun the other day and made accusations I later discovered to be baseless. I am so sorry about that."

And so you should be. "Perhaps you should have asked Emma to attend the sports day in the first place." The apology hardly made up for how he had made her feel. "She was there anyway, so it wouldn't have been any trouble for her."

He raised his eyebrows. "Sorry it was such an imposition."

"It wasn't… of course, it wasn't." Belatedly, she noted Jeremy watching her with round eyes, clearly wondering what they were talking about.

"You ran really well, Jeremy. That was a great effort."

"I heard you yelling, so I ran faster."

"I'm glad I helped. That made it a good team effort. Hi five." She held up her hand and Jeremy smacked it enthusiastically.

"Dad," Jeremy said, tugging at his father's arm, "Alyssa could have breakfast with us."

At that point, Phillip emerged from the café, bearing two steaming mugs of coffee and with the menu cards tucked under one arm.

"Here you are… double-shot flat white, extra hot, just as you like it. I remembered the skinny milk as well."

He lowered the mugs to the table and gave an enquiring look at the man and boy standing beside her.

"Another time, Jeremy," Max said. "Alyssa has made other arrangements. We'd better get our shopping done." He nodded in her direction. "I'll see you around, Alyssa." He didn't wait to be introduced, but giving Jeremy a nudge, headed off in the direction of the stalls.

"Who was that?" Phillip asked. "Surly chap. Friend of yours?"

"He's a client," Alyssa replied. "He's also working on the development project I mentioned last night, so we've had a few clashes."

"That explains the vibes I got from the man. I thought I must have trodden on his patch, but it was you he was glowering at. Glad to see you know how to keep the local yokels in their place."

It wasn't like that, but she didn't want to discuss Max with Phillip. There was no reason to mention him more than she already had.

Clean slate in the city, she said. No-one to draw her back, or words to that effect. Either she was lying or she was fooling herself. That guy had 'city' stamped all over him, and he sure as hell acted with a sense of proprietary.

"Dad… slow down."

Max paused and half-turned, allowing Jeremy to catch up.

"Who was that man?"

"I've no idea. Some friend of Alyssa's."

I thought *we* were her friends."

"So did I, mate. Alyssa probably has lots of friends. Paul and Jacinta… they're friends of hers too.'

"Okay." His son sounded doubtful, but didn't ask any more questions. They had stopped at one of the fruit stalls, and the assistant gave him a slice of apple from the sample plate, and eating took precedence over curiosity.

Max had been pleased when he spotted Alyssa sitting outside the café. He wasn't sure if she'd been deliberately avoiding his calls or if he'd rung at inconvenient times, but it gave him the opportunity of apologising in person. As a result of that interaction, he surmised she'd been avoiding him and she hadn't actually said she accepted the apology. He must have upset her badly. Thanks, Emma.

Whatever. She wasn't moping at home. Max thought back to their time at night on the headland. Just as well he'd only made a minor fool of himself. He needn't think about her any further.

13 – The Storm

PHILLIP STROLLED BACK to his hotel, while Alyssa returned home with her shopping.

"I might go for a walk along the beach later. I need to shove these goodies in the hotel fridge first, but the walk will do me good. Blow some fresh air into these lungs. Are you up for a drive this afternoon?"

He'd bought some cheese and olives after they finished breakfast, deciding it was probably a criminal offence to attend a market and not actually purchase anything. Alyssa had been waiting for him to put the hard word on her about their relationship, but he'd been remarkably chilled. It wasn't like the Phillip she knew at all. A modicum of self-preservation said she would be mad to spend the entire day with him, but then she felt mean. It didn't have to be all day, but no harm in going for a drive.

"I've a few domestic chores right now, but I can pick you up early afternoon and we can drive down the coast to Pt

Reilly. There is a winery you might like to visit along the way, and there are a couple of galleries in the town."

He shook his head with bemusement. "I can't remember when I last had a weekend like this. Why don't I pick you up instead. I remember the way to your aunt's house. You can sit back and be the tour guide."

Cars had always been more important to Phillip, and she suspected that he preferred his Audi to her Mazda, and always preferred being behind the wheel. Whatever. She was quite happy to be chauffeured. "Sure. Pick me up at two. You might need a jacket for late afternoon. The sea breezes come in then."

"You always were the more practical out of the two of us. I'll see you then."

She hadn't lied. She did have some chores to do, but she needed some time away from him as well. He was behaving like the man she'd first met and had been highly attracted to, but she felt as though she were waiting for the axe to fall. Surely, he would raise the issue of selling the house and renegotiating their relationship?

Alyssa made herself a cup of tea, and took it out onto the deck with a notepad. Tiger followed her out, and sat in the sun putting himself through an elaborate washing routine. Making notes always gave her clarity on confronting a decision or a problem. She had to be clear about her needs before Phillip raised any issues.

Did she still want to sell the house? Yes, because she didn't want to live there again, knowing what had happened there in her absence. She no longer felt the same attachment for the place, although still grieving her initial hopes and dreams.

Would she contemplate resuming her relationship with Phillip? Underlying that question was the issue of his motivation. If he was using her to improve his career prospects, as Charlotte had indicated, then no. If he was genuine in his affection and love for her, maybe. If he could promise that he wouldn't stray again… and here her note-taking stalled.

Comments about a leopard not changing its spots ran through her head. She thought back over the years of their relationship. There were times when she'd had doubts about his fidelity, but always he'd convinced her that she was imagining things, or else being unreasonably jealous. She'd chosen to ignore the niggling feelings—after all, he'd stayed with her, but she didn't want to have those doubts.

Perhaps he wouldn't pressure her at all. Perhaps he was happy that she'd moved on and genuinely just wanted to remain friends. Maybe he told the truth when he referred to closure. On that basis, she would simply enjoy the weekend for old time's sake.

The Audi pulled up in the driveway dead on two o'clock. Phillip looked relaxed and sporty with his straw fedora and aviator sunglasses. He stood leaning against the side of the car as Alyssa came down the stairs from the deck level to meet him.

"Ready to go?"

He moved around to the passenger side of the car and opened the door so she could slide inside. He opened the sunroof letting in the fresh air on the drive. The car stereo produced superior sound, and he cranked that up also so that most of the other drivers must have heard his music selection as well. Some things never changed. He'd always liked his toys, and only the best.

She directed him to the winery she'd mentioned earlier, and they sampled the wines and browsed the vineyard shop, stocking a range of local produce. Phillip bought two bottles of merlot, and they continued on down to Pt Reilly. They found an art exhibition in the town hall, organized by members of a regional art society and browsed the antique shops in town. Alyssa found a pretty cup, saucer and plate set, and decided they would be just the thing for Sunday brunch on the deck.

Phillip bought them each an ice cream from a kiosk on the foreshore, and they strolled out along the jetty as they ate. The tide was coming in, and the late afternoon breeze whipped up a swell in the water. Seagulls arced in the air over the jetty, no doubt looking for any food scraps that might come their way, and a lone pelican sat on the railings, oblivious to the cameras pointed in its direction.

Evening approached by the time they completed their jetty stroll and arrived back on the shore and in front of the Commodore Hotel.

"Fancy a drink?" Phillip asked, nodding towards the pub. The white, art deco style building stood out in stark contrast to surrounding buildings, and was a favourite with tourists and locals alike.

The afternoon had been a pleasant interlude and Alyssa couldn't think of a good reason why not. She had no other obligations. "You're driving, so up to you."

"I'll take that as a yes."

In spite of it being a Saturday evening, there was still a table available in the bar. Phillip ordered a light ale for himself, and a glass of rosé for her and they settled back as the evening closed in.

Phillip raised his glass to her in toast. "I've really enjoyed today—thank you. It's so long since I've has such a relaxed weekend. I should do it more often."

"It's good for the stress levels." She deliberately didn't ask how things were going at work, knowing what Charlotte had told her. "Perhaps you're due for a holiday."

"Maybe, but I'm not inclined to take one on my own. I'm more of a social person, as you obviously know."

Was that his way of telling her that his new lady friend hadn't stuck around? Alyssa wasn't going to ask about that either. They ended up staying for dinner at the hotel as well. Instead of another round of drinks in the bar, Phillip suggested they move into the dining room instead, and it seemed churlish to refuse. He hadn't raised any of the questions she anticipated, so she had worried over nothing.

Phillip dropped her back at Seaclusion shortly after ten. He peered at the steps leading up from the driveway to the deck. "Shall I walk you up to the front door?"

"Don't be silly. The security lights will come on automatically, and I tear up and down those steps several times a day."

"I was just joking," he said, reaching out and brushing a strand of hair from her face. "I have to leave early in the morning, but I'm glad I got to spend this time with you. I know you're back in Adelaide from time to time, so look me up when you do. What we've shared together has been too special to just discard."

He leaned forward and gently brushed her lips with his, leaving her with mixed feelings. She opened the car door and jumped out before leaning back in to speak to him. "I've enjoyed today. I'll be in touch."

She shut the car door and almost ran up the steps. He sat in the car with the engine idling until the lights came on and she was clearly at the top. He gave a quick toot of farewell, then reversed out of the driveway. She watched as this tail lights travelled along the road and then disappeared around the bend. Then, she went inside and shut the door.

The next day being Sunday, Alyssa had the opportunity of using her vintage porcelain set out on the deck as she ate her breakfast. Looking out over the headland, she saw Max's car first, and then his head just visible over the shrubbery as he moved around the site. She had no idea if he was checking his cameras or recording some other information in relation to the land. Whatever he was doing, she had no interest in connecting with him.

Picking up her cup and saucer, she quickly moved inside and joined Tiger on a comfy chair in the lounge room. She had a new book from the library and was keen to read it. She was barely ten pages in when her phone rang. She glanced at the screen. Jacinta.

"So, who was that guy you wandered through Pt Reilly with yesterday?" She asked the question half with curiosity and half with amusement in her voice.

148

"What? Were you spying on me?"

"Jacinta laughed. Not exactly. I was coming out of the supermarket and I saw you and some cool-looking dude heading into the art exhibition."

"That was Phillip, my ex."

"He didn't look very ex to me."

"It's a long story, but he's very ex and after this weekend, continues to be ex. It was a pleasant interlude though after a shitty week."

"Yeah, Paul did tell me something about that. I only got the abridged version though."

Alyssa recognised a request for more information when she heard it. "It's another long story, but I attended Jeremy's sports day because Max had a work commitment in the city. While I was distracted by a phone call, a friend of Max's called Emma lured Jeremy away, telling Max I had abandoned the boy. She knew exactly where I was, and so did Jeremy. I put it down to malevolent interference. Max bought the whole sorry story and blasted me when he found out."

She heard Jacinta draw in her breath.

"I put it down to a green-eyed monster myself. What's wrong with Max?"

"She doesn't need to worry because I'm not interested. Max apologised yesterday, but I wasn't in a very forgiving mood. At least he knows he blew it."

"I'm sorry things are strained between you. I did think you two could be a good match."

Alyssa chose to ignore that comment. "Aside from that, there's a Council meeting scheduled for the week after next. The project on the headland will be on the agenda, so Max and

I will be on opposite sides of the fence. He works for the developer, and I'm opposing the project."

"Well, you know what they say… opposites attract."

"I'm not sure who these mythical *they* are, but they've got it wrong in this instance."

Jacinta just laughed. "Whatever. Drop in for a coffee sometime. We can talk about other things besides men and their failings, like what books you've read lately and if you've seen any good films."

"It's a deal."

ȣ

The committee formed in opposition to the headland development took up a bit of time over the next few days, but otherwise it was a regular week. Alyssa felt as though she had worked at Densley and Associates forever, and her work schedule followed a predictable routine. She knew where to find the stationery items she needed, and she and Jodie had developed a comfortable working relationship. The work was just varied enough to maintain her interest.

The tension stakes were higher in relation to the headland. Knowing the Council was about to make a decision on the development, the committee ramped up their media campaign against it and made sure there was plenty of social media coverage. Anyone who stood still long enough was persuaded to sign a petition condemning the proposal, and various meetings were held to canvass community attitudes. Not everyone was against it. Some thought that the increased commercial activity would be good for local businesses and also employment.

"You have to think about our young people," one resident remarked. "If they can't get employment here, they'll have to leave, and without them Sandy Bay will just become a giant retirement village."

"We're not all that old," Alyssa protested, but it was the most common argument in support of the project, and one which she had to refute tactfully. There were other employment options, but they needed to be explored in greater depth.

"What are the results of the environmental investigation?" one of the committee members asked.

"We don't know yet," Alyssa replied regretfully. If she'd stayed on better terms with Max, he might have told her. It would have been useful to know. "That document remains the property of the developers, as they commissioned it, but it will probably be tabled at the council meeting."

"But don't you know the guy who was preparing the report? You could ask him."

"I know him, yes, but not well enough to ask him to break client confidentiality. That would not be a great move for a lawyer."

The committee member sniffed and rolled his eyes, as though to say he didn't see the problem but didn't push it further. Alyssa ignored him and checked the time. She had to cram as much into her lunch hour as she could. Time to go.

Paul wandered into her office mid-week with a nonchalant air that would fool precisely no-one, and perched himself on a corner of her desk. He enquired about progress on a particular file, and appeared engrossed in the state of his fingernails before broaching the subject which had probably brought him in there.

"I hope you're being diplomatic in how you're dealing with the council staff over this headland development. Council occasionally engages us on legal matters. It's not necessarily a huge part of our business, but I wouldn't like to lose that income source."

Alyssa felt herself flushing. She hated to think that she was causing Paul anxiety over her involvement with the protest. "Paul, I'm involved as an individual. People may know where I work, but I'm careful not to give the impression that I'm speaking on behalf of Densley and Associates, because I'm not."

"Of course, I wouldn't have assumed otherwise, I just wanted to make sure… you know… This is a small town and people make assumptions and before long, it's accepted as fact."

Great. The joys of small-town living. This wouldn't be such an issue in the city. She dragged up her most reassuring smile. "Don't worry, I'll make sure my behaviour is squeaky clean."

When she drove home that evening, the conversation with Paul played over in her mind. Would it always be like this in Sandy Bay, having to be careful what she said and did? She'd experienced freedom from city pressures since moving to the coastal town, but privacy could be the cost. It was a juggling exercise.

As she pulled up in the driveway, she saw Tiger sitting in the window, looking down at her. Oh, for the uncomplicated life of a cat. That's what she would be in her next life.

৵

Storms were forecast for the weekend. Batton down the hatches. Alyssa scanned the deck for loose items, and folded the umbrella erected over the outdoor table. She took the cushions inside, and figured she had done all she reasonably could.

The wind hit on the Saturday evening. It swept in from the ocean and shook the leaves on the trees so that they rained on the roof. Alyssa peered out through the windows, straining in the fading light to see what was happening. The sea had been whipped up into an angry froth, and when she poked her head out the door to check that nothing had come loose outside, she could hear the surf pounding against the cliff.

She retreated inside, drew the curtains, and made a cup of hot chocolate. It would be a night to shut the weather out. She hoped all the local fishermen were safely ashore and not out at sea. Mary's car occupied the garage, so she had to leave hers in the open. Hail wasn't forecast, so as long as it withstood the rain, it would be all right.

Around ten that evening the rain started. There were occasional fat drops at first and then the dam broke and water teamed down in an absolute torrent, drumming on the iron roof. Hearing the television was impossible so she turned if off. Tiger woke up from his evening snooze and yowled in protest. In the end, she went to bed, with a torch on the bedside table in case the power was cut. Tiger snuggled up close, and they both woke periodically, listening to the torment outside before drifting off again.

Usually, she woke to a variety of bird songs, but not the next morning. A weird silence greeting her when she gingerly slipped out of bed and drew the bedroom curtains. Amazingly, she'd slept in, perhaps because of the frequent interruptions during the night. The sky was grey, and when she wandered to the front part of the house, she could see that the sea, now a turgid grey/blue colour, still smashed against the shore.

She walked outside to do a quick assessment of the impact of the storm. The garden was littered with leaves and small branches ripped from shrubs and trees. Her car seemed to be fine, and that was a consolation but she wouldn't be driving it anywhere for a while. A large, white cedar tree grew at the bottom of the driveway, at least it had. It had come down during the storm, and now lay across the driveway. Her car was going nowhere. She was trapped.

14 – The Aftermath

ALYSSA STARED WITH dismay at the chaos at the end of the driveway. She shook her head slightly hoping to shake her brain into gear. How to deal with this mess? She needed a shower and a cup of coffee. Then she could work out where and how to get help. From her quick glance around the property, the tree was the major issue she needed to deal with. A broom and a wheelbarrow could sort out everything else.

Bliss. The water was still hot. To not have that stream of hot water in the bathroom would have reduced her to tears. She dressed in jeans, a windcheater, and sturdy boots. She would look for work gloves in the garden shed. After coffee. Breakfast would be good too, but she could eat later. She only got as far as the kitchen when she heard an unmistakable noise. A chainsaw—a revving, screaming chainsaw that shattered the early morning silence.

From her vantage point on the deck, she saw a man clad in hi-vis vest and wearing a hard hat cutting some of the smaller branches from the fallen tree. The State Emergency

Service must have arrived. Perhaps a neighbour rang them. She ran down the steps to investigate, grateful that her tree was already receiving attention. It must be a really busy morning for them.

She stood to one side, well clear of the action, until the man spotted her. He turned off the saw, and nodded at her, moving his earmuff away from one ear. Only then did she recognise him. Max was under the hard hat and behind the safety goggles.

"What are you doing here?" As she spoke, she realized she didn't sound very gracious.

"What does it look like? I'm chopping up this tree."

"But why?"

He jerked his head behind him. "I came down to the headland early to check on the monitoring stations. I saw that the tree was down and knew you'd be blocked in, so went home and got the chainsaw." He paused, and pulled a face. "You don't object?"

"No, but… the SES people would probably do that if I asked them."

"Sure, they'd do it, but not for a while. There are trees down all over town, plus a few fences and some rooves have blown off as well. You'd be waiting a long time."

Alyssa ran her fingers through her hair, conscious that she hadn't brushed it. Her fingers snagged in the tangled curls. He was right.

"Um… thank you. That's very thoughtful of you." She glanced around, looking for Jeremy. "Is Jeremy here?"

"He's sitting in the car with some games. It's safer there."

"He can come up to the house. I'll set him up with a video, or he can keep playing his games if he wants. I'll leave him with some food and drink and then put on some gloves and join you. I'll stack all the material you've cut up to one side."

He nodded, with his face showing minimal expression. "That would be helpful. It will be quicker that way." He glanced over at the car where she could now see Jeremy's head, slumped back against the seat. "I'll ask Jeremy if he wants to stay in the car or would prefer the house. He can see me here, so he might be more comfortable sitting in the car."

Alyssa shrugged, but after a quick conversation, the small boy jumped out of the car, stuffing his notepad in his backpack.

"Hi Alyssa. Dad says I can see inside your house."

"Sure. Follow me. You'll have Tiger to keep you company, but you'll be able to see us working down here."

You've got a tiger?" His eyes widened with excitement.

"Come and see. He's very friendly."

She led the way up the stairs and made the introduction between the boy and feline. She showed him where the bathroom was, and also pointed out that he could keep an eye on his father from the deck, though it was warmer inside in the lounge. She then quickly dropped a slice of bread in the toaster and made two mugs of coffee and a mug of hot chocolate. She needed sustenance before embarking on strenuous activity.

She left Jeremy with the hot drink and instructions to call to her from the deck if he needed anything. Clutching the two mugs of coffee, she made her way down the steps and then the driveway to where Max worked at a steady pace. She'd found earmuffs in the shed along with some gloves, and was grateful for that. The scream of the chainsaw motor was enough to send anyone deaf.

She stood in a position where Max could readily see her and held up the mug of coffee to catch his attention. He switched off the motor and peeled off the goggles and muffs.

"Thanks. That's just what I need. Jeremy's okay?"

"He's fine. He knows he can see you if he needs reassurance."

After gulping down the coffee, they got stuck into the tree. Max worked solidly, cutting off the smaller branches first before tackling the larger limbs and then the trunk. The larger pieces of timber had to be cut into lengths that they could both handle, stacking it all on the footpath. The resultant pile filled the width of the footpath but kept the driveway clear.

They worked well as a team, speaking little but anticipating what the other needed or was about to do.

"Max took off his earmuffs and goggles, wiping his brow with the back of his hand. "I reckon you could call the Council now and they'll arrange for this lot to be picked up and taken to the green waste depot."

"I'll do that first thing in the morning. For now, we'd better go and check on your son, and I'll make us something to eat. You must be famished after all that work. I know I am."

He checked the controls on the chainsaw and then put it in the back of the car. "It has been a long time since breakfast. I don't want to impose though."

"Well, breakfast was a non-event for me this morning, so I'm certainly due for a snack. We need to check on Jeremy anyway."

The child had been incredibly quiet, aside from coming out onto the deck a couple of times and waving at them. When they climbed the stairs, they found that he and Tiger were curled up on the lounge, watching one of the videos she had provided.

"Hey, kiddo, are you hungry?" Alyssa asked.

He nodded without looking at her, not wanting to take his eyes off the screen.

"Sit," she directed Max. "My repertoire in the kitchen is not extensive, but I can produce something edible. Give me a few minutes."

After casting an eye over his son, Max perched himself on a stool by the kitchen bench, watching as she rummaged in the cupboards and dumped a bowl and whisk on the benchtop, followed by flour, eggs, milk, baking powder, butter, sugar and milk.

"This looks like a lot of trouble. You don't need to do this."

"Yes, I do. It's Sunday morning. That calls for Sunday morning food. Pancakes coming up."

She mixed the ingredients, leaving the batter to settle while she found the crepe pan and set it on the hotplate to heat. She dropped a blob of butter into the pan, swirling it around as it melted, frothed and bubbled. Before it started to brown, she poured in the first of the mixture. The buttery smell from the pan had her salivating. The slice of toast earlier had in no way sufficed for breakfast.

"Can I help? Is there anything I can do?" Max sounded bemused as he watched the flurry of activity occurring before him.

"Probably not. You'd only get in the way." She filled the kettle and flicked the switch. "I mean that nicely, of course."

She wondered about doing a theatrical pancake flip, but then opted for the spatula to turn it. Just this time, she would probably drop it, or it would end up on the ceiling. For some reason she hadn't identified, she didn't want to appear a culinary klutz in front of Max. She had never imagined him being in her kitchen. She was acutely aware of his eyes on her, watching her every move.

"The development proposal is going before Council on Monday," he finally said. "At this stage, they are looking for concept approval. I should warn you that I haven't found any convincing environmental reason why it shouldn't proceed. There are issues that can be argued, such as loss of sand dunes and local habitat, and then the visual amenity aspect, but those are not irrefutable arguments." He crossed his arms and leaned back on the stool. "I'm still monitoring the site, but haven't found anything yet that would put an immediate stop to the project."

She took a moment to digest this news, tipping the pancake out onto a plate and adding more batter into the pan. "I'm sorry to hear that. I won't give up the fight though. If Council votes to take it to the next step, I'll take our opposition to the Environmental Resource and Development Court. The protesters are determined to see it through."

He nodded. "I thought that would be the case. I just thought you should know. I haven't recommended in favour of the project, just presented the facts as I found them."

She glanced at him and noticed that he was staring at her, monitoring for her reaction. The light streaming in through the adjacent window caught the green of his eyes, giving them unusual clarity of colour. Framed with dark eyelashes, they made her incredibly jealous. Not fair that a man should have mesmerizing eyes like that.

She sighed. "I know you had a job to do. I just wish it hadn't been for that purpose."

He bit his lip, then massaged his jaw with one hand. Was speaking to her that hard? He stopped the massaging and placed both hands on the counter in front of him.

"I don't want to dwell on it, but I am truly sorry for the misunderstanding the other week."

She dismissed his concern with a flap of her hand. "Forget it. I already have." That was a lie, but there was little to be gained from harbouring grudges. After all, she wouldn't be staying in Sandy Bay forever. She would see out her contract with Paul, but would ask her connections to keep her in mind for any openings that arose in the city. Probably her old firm would take her back, but that might be a regressive step. She would look for new opportunities.

She flipped the next pancake and made their drinks, slipping between the cupboards, the kettle and the counter top. She passed the drinks over to him. "Put these on the table. You need to call Jeremy as well."

While father and son were engaged in quiet conversation, no doubt around the need to pause the video, she set the table with plates, butter, strawberry jam, cream, and maple syrup. Lucky Mary kept a well-stocked pantry. By the time Max returned to the kitchen with Jeremy in tow, she had a pile of hot pancakes sitting on the table, and another sizzling in the pan.

"There's more batter left so we can definitely have seconds or thirds. We should start on these while they're still warm."

"Are they for us?" Jeremy asked, with eyes reflecting his delight. "Dad never makes us pancakes."

"I do so. Don't tell stories."

"Yeah, but not like this. Yours are usually burnt."

"You can cook your own in future," Max muttered.

"No, Alyssa can come and cook them for us."

"This is a one-off, mate." Max ruffled his son's hair. "Alyssa can't spend all her time with us. She has other friends."

"Yeah, I remember. You told me, like Paul and Jacinta and that man we saw her with last week."

Max coloured slightly and didn't look at her, but handed his son a paper napkin. "Something like that. Wipe your face. You're covered in sticky syrup."

Interesting. They took note of Phillip when we were at the market.

As a diversionary tactic, Max's action with the napkin worked, and conversation moved onto more general topics. The school term had ended, and Jeremy was full of chatter about the Christmas holidays, and what presents he might find under the tree.

"Are you getting a tree?" he asked Alyssa.

The question threw her off balance. Christmas wasn't on her radar this year. Mary was away, and she wouldn't be spending it with Phillip this year. She would probably take herself out to a local hotel for lunch, rather than sit home by herself. Maybe Charlotte could come down for the promised visit.

"I hadn't planned on getting one."

"Alyssa could have lunch with us on Christmas Day, couldn't she dad?"

Alyssa broke in quickly. "That's very kind of you to suggest that Jeremy, but you'll probably spend the day with your grandparents."

"They won't mind if you come too." He looked at her with the youthful assurance that most things in life are simple. Alyssa looked to Max in mute appeal.

Max shrugged. "He's right, you'd be most welcome, but I don't know what plans you already have. Perhaps you're planning on spending Christmas in the city with friends? Don't feel pressured or obligated."

That was a rather off-hand statement. Was he hoping she wouldn't come, but didn't want to say that? "I haven't confirmed any plans yet. I'll let you know. Anyone for another pancake?"

Max was relieved that he found minimal damage at the headland, following the storm. Some branches were on the ground, and clearly a massive weather event had gone through, but the installations were all intact. It was only as he turned to go and looked up towards Seaclusion that he saw the tree across the driveway. There was no way Alyssa would be able to move that on her own. She might not even know about it yet. She was probably still in bed.

He could make his way on foot around the tree and go up to the house and let her know, but after their last interaction, he hesitated to do that. She'd made it clear on that occasion that she wanted little to do with him and he didn't blame her. He would have to give the SES a call.

On the other hand, he could go home and get the chainsaw from the shed, come back, and start cutting up and clearing the tree himself. She would wait hours for the SES, and they might not even get to her today. He ruminated on the options during the drive home, and by the time he pulled up, he realized that he was getting the chainsaw and that had been his intention all along. It would go part way towards making up for the accusations he'd leveled at her.

Back at the entrance to Seaclusion, he left Jeremy in the car, and reviewed the task ahead of him. Close up, it looked like a lot of tree. He began to doubt his decision, but now that he was here, he needed to get on with it. He donned his safety gear, started the motor, and approached the first branches, brandished the rotating teeth before him with grim determination.

He wasn't surprised when Alyssa suddenly appeared, looking slightly tousled and bewildered as though not long out of bed. She sounded quite grumpy, which made her decision to join him more surprising. It was good of her to let Jeremy sit inside the house instead of cramped up in the car. He watched the two of them as they climbed the stairs to the deck, Jeremy chatting all the way. The boy didn't usually take to people in the way he had to Alyssa.

Pancakes! It was a Sunday morning tradition he hadn't bothered about in a long time. He meant to, for Jeremy's sake, but kept forgetting, and as the kid said, he sometimes burnt them, or else they were not quite cooked in the middle. Hard to say what was worse. After a while he stopped doing it.

At least Alyssa seemed to have forgiven him. She would forget about that though if and when the council approved the development application, which he was reasonably sure now that they would. He'd picked up whispers here and there about the likely outcome. She had stared at him when he told her, not saying anything for a moment, before flipping the next pancake. She pursed her lips before saying very decisively, "I won't give up this fight". It surprised him to realise that he would have been very disappointed if she did.

What she didn't mention, or rather *who* she didn't mention, was the man she was breakfasting with the previous weekend. He half expected that when Jeremy spontaneously invited her to spend Christmas with them, that she would say she already had an invitation back in the city. He confirmed that she would be most welcome; who would want to spend Christmas alone? but she remained non-committal. The impression she gave was *I'm considering my options.* Fair enough.

He checked the time on his phone. "Jeremy mate, we've been here long enough. Time we got out of Alyssa's hair. She probably has other stuff to do. Gather up your things and put them back in your bag."

Jeremy pouted and gave a theatrical sigh before sliding off his chair and doing as his father asked while Max stood and waited.

"Jeremy, I think you have something to say to Alyssa."

The boy dutifully stood in front of her. "Thank you for letting me sit in your house. Thank you for the pancakes." His eyes slid over to his father and then back again to her. "Dad makes pizza too. He doesn't always burn them like the pancakes. You could come and have pizza at our house."

Max noted the bemused smile. She seemed to relate to his son better than to him, but then, Jeremy extended more invitations.

"Maybe I will," she said. "Whenever it's a convenient time for your father, and he's not taken by surprise."

"Tonight, dad?"

This child is persistent. "Sure. Depends on Alyssa." He turned an inquiring look in her direction. "There are no guarantees about burnt or not burnt, but if you are free this evening, you're most welcome."

This time, she looked directly at him. He had the impression she was trying not to laugh. "Sounds like an offer too good to refuse. Tell me where and when, and I'll be there."

Holy shite—she was actually coming. He felt ridiculously pleased. She wouldn't stay in this mood for long, but for now he would make the most of it. Now all he had to do was turn out a culinary masterpiece. How hard could that be?

15 – Pizza

ALYSSA LOOKED OUT over the bay and pulled her jacket tighter around her body. Dark clouds hung low on the horizon, and the temperature had settled lower than expected for this time of year. The wind had settled to a gentle breeze, but the earth still had a smell of damp peat and moldering leaves. She had completed a tour of the garden and was relieved to find the damage was minimal. The cedar tree must have taken the brunt of the storm. Mary would be sad about that when she learned what had happened.

She knew she would have been in strife if Max hadn't turned up with his chainsaw. That was the thing about small towns; people took note of what happened around them and pitched in when help was needed. Putting aside their differences, she was grateful to him, but still had surprised herself in accepting his invitation to join him and Jeremy for pizza.

She put it down to the pancake effect. Pancakes on a Sunday morning could put anyone in a good mood. That and the fact that she had decided that her stay in Sandy Bay was a temporary sojourn. She would make the most of it while she was here, and leave town at the end of her tenure with no regrets.

Early evening saw her ringing the doorbell at Max's house, bearing a bottle of locally bottled merlot, and a tub of honeycomb ice cream. She heard the thud of feet approaching the door on the other side, and when it swung open, Jeremy stood there beaming at her.

"Dad's in the kitchen. He's cooking."

"I approve of that. Every dad should be in the kitchen."

Jeremy cast her a confused look as she followed him into the kitchen/dining room. Max had tucked a tea towel into the top of his trousers as a makeshift apron, and had a smear of flour on his forehead. He had already rolled out the dough, and was tugging it onto shape over two pizza trays. The urge to reach out and brush the flour from his face was almost irresistible, but he would probably just put more there before he was finished. Alyssa placed the bottle of merlot on the kitchen bench, and waved the ice-cream at him.

"Okay if I put this in the freezer until we need it?"

"Sure. Then you can tell me if you have any intolerances or food aversions. I've got all the topping ingredients ready, and thought we could do an adult version and a kid version."

"I'll eat most things. I love anchovies, and don't object to pineapple on pizzas. I'm never going to object to a meal someone else has cooked."

He grimaced. "You might want to wait until you see the end result before voicing that opinion. Shall I open the bottle? I find a glass of wine can help the cooking process."

"You're busy. I'll open it, if you point me in the direction of the glasses."

He pointed to one of the cupboards and she found a couple of wine glasses. She cracked open the screw top, and inhaled the fruity aroma. It smelled good. She poured a couple of glasses of wine, and after setting one in front of Max, sat down on one of the kitchen chairs. Jeremy, Max assured her, as he smoothed tomato paste over the pizza bases, was happy with a glass of water.

She wasn't allowed to sit for long. Jeremy dragged her into his room to show her his Lego truck, his books, and a variety of treasures, giving her a detailed explanation of each. When they returned to the kitchen, the two pizzas were in the oven and Max was tidying the mess he'd made including to his face.

"Smells good already," Alyssa said.

"Yeah, as long as he doesn't burn it," Jeremy said in a scornful tone.

Max flicked a tea towel at his son. "In future, you're in charge of cooking your own."

Alyssa noted that he had set the oven timer and he peaked inside the oven door every couple of minutes. Cooking time was short, and they were done to perfection when he slid them out of the oven and onto heat-resistant mats on the benchtop. He grabbed a pizza cutter, and expertly sliced the pizzas into neat triangles. The kid version featured lots of ham, cheese and pineapple, and the adult version was loaded with artichoke hearts, olives, anchovies and cherry bocconcini, plus some shreds of chicken. There were even some torn basil leaves. It impressed her that he had a herb garden.

Max directed them where to sit at the dining table, and plonked the pizza trays and their individual plates on the table, with instructions to 'help themselves'.

"I'll have some of that one, dad."

It amused Alyssa to see that Jeremy pointed to the adult pizza. She didn't blame him. It looked good. They both did, and smelled divine.

Jeremy sat with his elbows on the table, waving his greasy hands in the air. A smear of tomato sauce decorated his face. "Alyssa, have you made up your mind about Christmas? Dad could cook you pizza again."

She passed him a paper napkin. Pizza for Christmas lunch? Seafood and salad was more her style. "Not yet, you only asked me this morning. Can I let you know in a few days?"

"Jeremy, stop hassling Alyssa. She probably has her own plans for Christmas."

"Well, I've a few—"

The doorbell rang, cutting her off. Max glanced at his watch with a small frown. "It's a bit late for the Mormons or whoever to come knocking." He pushed back his chair while wiping his hands on a napkin and disappeared in the direction of the front door.

"Hi. I wondered if you had any damage in the storm last night? It was fierce at my place."

"No, we're fine. Thank you. We're just having dinner."

Alyssa recognised the visitor's voice. Emma. She had just enough time to compose herself before Jeremy twisted in his chair, and called out.

"Hi Aunty Emma. A tree came down at Alyssa's house and she cooked us pancakes."

Footsteps sounded in the hall.

"Oh, really? That sounds—"

She stood in the doorway to the kitchen, and stopped mid-sentence when she saw Alyssa sitting there. Max hovered behind her, with a look of anguish on his face.

"Sorry, I didn't realise you had a… a guest." She almost choked on the last word.

"Did you want some pizza?" Jeremy burbled happily. "Dad cooked it for Alyssa cos I said he sometimes burns them and Dad said he wouldn't. It's okay, he didn't this time."

The child was the only one oblivious to the atmosphere.

"Emma, how nice to see you again," Alyssa said, sarcastically emphasizing the word *nice*. A million things raced through her head that she would rather say. *Are you in the habit of kidnapping children? Are you a habitual liar? Just what is your problem?* She kept in mind that she was in Max's house, and clearly the two of them were good friends.

Emma flushed bright red. "Look, I won't stay." She focused on Max. "Perhaps you can cook me some pizza another time. I've always enjoyed your cooking and it's never been burned for me."

"Yes, of course. Another time," Max muttered, extending his arm towards the door as though that would usher her out more quickly. With a flat look in Alyssa's direction, the woman turned and left. A low conversation took place at the front door, but too soft for Alyssa to make out the words. Whatever it was, neither of them sounded very happy.

Alyssa topped up both of their wine glasses, surmising that when he was back at the table, Max might need a drink. Need was too strong a word for her, but she still swigged a mouthful. Max sat down again, staring at his now congealing pizza, as though it might reveal some magical insights about what was happening in his life. Jeremy continued eating his meal and intermittently chatting.

"Emma could have stayed… there's plenty of food. Usually she brings us food, doesn't she, Dad?"

Max reached for his wine. "Eat your tea, mate. You talk too much."

It was time to change the mood. "When you've both finished with pizza, there is some honeycomb ice cream in the freezer. I thought that might make a nice dessert."

Jeremy polished off the remainder of his food remarkably quickly, and without mentioning Emma again. Max produced some bowls and dished up the ice cream, after which they all adjourned to the lounge room. Jeremy persuaded Alyssa to join him in a game of Uno, until Max declared that it was time for bed.

"But it's too early."

"It's later than you think. Go and get your pyjamas on."

Alyssa interpreted Max's side of the conversation as meaning, *I would like some adult time now so you need to go to bed.* "Hurry up, Jeremy. I'll come and tuck you in once you're in bed. After that, I need to be going as well. It's a work day tomorrow."

Max shot her a grateful look and called out "Don't forget to clean your teeth," as Jeremy scampered down the passage to his room.

Alyssa kept her promise and slipped into the room and tucked the covers around the small boy. "Night, night, sleep tight, hope the bugs don't bite."

He giggled in response and to her surprise, reached up to wrap his arms around her neck and gave her a hug. "Thank you, Alyssa. I like you. Don't forget to come for Christmas."

"I like you too," she responded, deliberately avoiding the Christmas issue. She crept out of the room, after turning out the light. Max waited in the lounge, with a bottle of Drambuie and two small glasses on the coffee table in front of him. He had selected some music in her absence, and the combined voices of Andre Bocelli and Sarah Goodman filled the room.

"Thank you for doing that. You'll join me in a wee dram before you go?"

"I shouldn't, but just one."

"I can't think of any good reason why you shouldn't. A grown woman is entitled to a wee dram of Scotland's finest liqueur. You worked hard this morning as well."

He gestured towards the front picture windows at the front of the room. "The sky has cleared. All traces of the storm have disappeared. Aside from the upheaval to the vegetation, the scene out there looks crisp and clean."

They wandered towards the windows. Like all houses in Sandy Bay, his house had been angled in construction to make the most of the sea view. It wasn't better than the view she had from Seaclusion, but different, featuring more of the town lights, and the silhouette of the Norfolk Island pine trees that lined the Esplanade. The sky wasn't quite dark, given that the days were long at that time of year, but it had taken on an inky hue. The jetty stretched out into the sea in front of them, with security lighting illuminating its path.

Max opened the double doors leading out onto his patio. "The wind has dropped, so we can sit out here, if that's okay with you. We'll still be able to hear the music."

A couple of canvas-covered deck chairs sat on the patio. When she sat, her chair creaked ominously, but presumably it was safe if it was used regularly. A bevy of moths fluttered around the outside light, occasionally throwing themselves against the globe. Alyssa and Max sat in companionable silence for a while, admiring the view. As he promised, the music followed them outside. The rendition of Canto Della Terra was truly uplifting. Alyssa was impressed that Max had chosen it.

She took a sip of the amber liquid, and licked her lips, relishing the residual sweet taste. She had forgotten how good it could be. The spire on top of the town's church was illuminated with a sparkling cross, and throughout the town, coloured lights twinkled. It reminded Alyssa that Christmas was approaching. People put up their Christmas lights earlier each year, and some streets combined to put on festive displays, but she wasn't in the Christmas mood.

She didn't want to disappoint Jeremy, but nor did she want to intrude on him and his friends and family, and that might include Emma. She definitely didn't want to share any part of Christmas day with that woman.

She thought a couple of times that Max was about to say something, but if so, he must have had second thoughts—either that or he was struggling with what he wanted to say. She was aware of his close proximity. She could have sworn the hairs on her arms were standing up in response to an electric charge, but it was probably due to the light breeze that now played around the patio.

A Christmas beetle ran across the surface of the patio, with the light catching the iridescent colours on its back. She hadn't seen one in years, but remembered they were often around when she was a kid. She watched its progress, leaning sideways in her chair as it scuttled around the other side of Max and towards the protective cover of darkness. As beetles went, it was cute. She leaned a little further, trying to follow its path.

***

It felt good to relax like this after a long day and an early start. Max sipped his Drambuie reflectively. How long since I've sat outside like this with a woman? Clara was so sick before she died. Last time was when I wheeled her outside. Thinking back over the times he had been with Alyssa, except for when she prepared his will, she hadn't asked any questions about Clara. He liked that. She hadn't pried about his marriage either. Their relationship—if you could call it that—was in the here and now, not rooted in the past.

He listened for calls from Jeremy's room, but all was quiet. He must have gone to sleep quickly. Thank goodness for that. On occasions, bedtime was a drawn-out process. He noticed a Christmas beetle running a crazy path past his feet. He drew his feet back so as not to impede its progress. As he did, he caught movement out of the corner of his eye. Before he had time to react, Alyssa's chair tilted precariously to one side and the weathered timber framework folded beneath her.

Alyssa and the remains of the chair ended in a tumbled heap on the ground.

"Alyssa! Are you all right? Grab my hand."

She looked dazed and stared up at him in confusion. "Give me a moment—I'm fine, just winded."

"God, I'm so sorry. I hope nothing's broken."

"Only the chair, I think."

She brushed off the palms of her hands and began awkwardly to lever herself up. "I think I spilled my drink."

"I'll buy you a bottle," he said and reached down to grasp her beneath her armpits and hauled her to her feet. "Are you sure you're okay?" He held her in a firm grip as though concerned that if he let go, her legs would fold beneath her. She stared up at him, her face flushed and eyes bright. Her chest brushed against his, and he wasn't sure if he imagined it or not, but could feel her heart beating. Perhaps it was his own he could feel, ricocheting within his rib cage in a crazy rhythm.

Her lips parted as though she was about to speak, but no words came. She licked them, with the tip of her pink tongue sweeping over her top lip. Would she taste of Drambuie? Her eyes followed him with a challenging stare as he lowered his mouth to hers and softly kissed her lips. She did.

"Are you trying to kiss it better?" she husked. "I think you need to do more than that."

He exhaled with a soft moan and moving his hands to grasp her more firmly, kissed her again with more heat. This time she kissed him back. The heat-level increased a notch when she slid her hands around his waist, and tucked them inside the waistband of his jeans.

When they surfaced for air, her lips had taken on a bruised and rosy hue. "Was this part of an elaborate plan?" she asked, eyebrows slightly raised. "Rather than give me a collapsible chair, you could simply have asked to kiss me."

As if he would have done that. Kissing her had not been on his mind, but now that he had, he wondered why not? Asking her would have been a helluva lot smarter than dumping a lawyer on the ground and risking a claim for damages.

"I didn't mean… it's never happened… I didn't realise the chair was so rickety."

She threw back her head and laughed. "I'm teasing you. It was my fault. Deck chairs are not stable if you lean sideways on them, though I do think this chair was nearing the end of its useful life." She looked up at him coyly, a totally Lady Di look. "Are you going to kiss me again?"

"I would, absolutely, but standing out here under the light, we're on show for all the neighbours. Perhaps we should move inside."

She nodded with a hint of sadness in her expression. "Emma might see us, you mean. You're right. It's a public display. I blame the Drambuie, but it tasted so nice." She ran her tongue over her upper lip again.

He held open the door leading back into the house. "I'll give you another, seeing as you threw the last drink over the patio."

"Thanks, but I'd better go. If that's what happens with one glass of Drambuie, what will happen if I have two?"

I'd love to find out. Max kept that thought to himself. She turned to face him when they were inside again, and he reached out and pulled her closer towards him. The allure of a warm, female body close to his was a sensation he'd almost forgotten, but now that she was in his arms, he wanted much more. Dammit, it wasn't just any woman. Something about Alyssa got under his skin, and if he was honest with himself, it had from that night at Paul and Jacinta's. Of all possible women, he had to be attracted to this one.

She looked up at him with a knowing expression, as though reading his mind. If only he could read hers. She reached up and kissed him lightly, holding the side of his face as she did. He could have sworn there was an electric vibration at the place of her touch.

With a regretful sigh, Alyssa disengaged herself from his embrace. She picked up the bag she'd brought with her and moved towards the front door. "Thank you for pizza, and of course thank you again for coming to my rescue this morning. That tree would probably still be there if you hadn't done that." She stopped at the door and turned to face him. "Max, I should let you know I'm not planning on staying in Sandy Bay when this contract is over. Despite my initial reservations, I do like you, and Jeremy's a great kid, but my future is up in the air. Don't bank on me being here long term."

Receiving you loud and clear. Max cleared his throat. "I wasn't making any assumptions, and like I said, nothing that happened this evening was planned. I don't regret it though."

Tapping him lightly in a farewell gesture, she turned and headed out to her car. The outside security light came on, and as she opened the car door, she looked back at him with an enigmatic expression that he hoped wasn't regret. She waved goodbye, and slid behind the wheel. He stood there watching as she reversed down the driveway and then kept watching as the tail-lights disappeared up the road.

He had no idea where this association with Alyssa was going. She hadn't said anything about the man she'd been having breakfast with, and whoever it was, they appeared to be on intimate terms. He had no desire to make a fool of himself. Life was complicated already, without adding more drama to the mix. There was something about Alyssa Finchley though that appealed. Whether it was her dedication and intensity, or her mercurial nature, he had no idea.

Of course, she came in a very attractive package, and he wasn't blind to that either. He rubbed his hand over his chin, feeling again in his mind the impact of her lips on his. He wondered what it would be like to kiss her again, away from the lights and prying eyes; to slowly unbutton her blouse and kiss the soft, silky skin between her breasts, and then her breasts themselves.

He shook his head. Keep your feet on the ground, Max, and your dick in your pants. Jeremy has to be your priority, and pursuing a relationship with no future will do neither of us any good. Especially when she's not going to hang around.

16 – Take it to Court

SHE'D HAD DIFFICULTY sleeping the previous night, with thoughts about storms, trees, and Max intruding when she closed her eyes and tried to relax. Sandy Bay was supposed to be a refuge from complicated relationships. The last thing she needed was to become entangled in another. Concerns about the development proposal superimposed themselves over her thoughts about Max, and then she worried about the impact her activism might have on Paul's business. By the time she dragged herself into the office, she felt a total wreck, and it was only Monday!

Jodie took one look at her and tsked sympathetically. "It was a bad storm, wasn't it? You look like you haven't slept for a week. Was there much damage?"

Alyssa regarded the receptionist over the rim of her coffee mug. "Do I look that bad? No, don't answer. I can guess. A tree came down across the driveway, but Max Saunders helped to cut it up and remove it. That reminds me... I must ring the Council about getting it picked up by green waste."

"Max Saunders… how come he cut it up for you?"

Warning signals flashed for Alyssa. Gossip could be all over town if she didn't choose her reply carefully. "He was being neighbourly. People are like that in small towns." She disappeared into her office before more questions followed. The week would be challenging enough as it was. She had to put her tumbling thoughts aside and focus on the day's work… for now.

The discussion relating to the resort development at the council meeting that evening was held in confidence, given the commercial nature of the report. Alyssa had expected that, and knew that even when the minutes of the meeting were ratified and made public, only the motion and resolution would be printed, but not the supporting detail. The grapevine she had cultivated told her the result before the minutes were officially released. Max's prediction had been correct. The project concept had been approved in principle, subject to further investigations. The developers had been given the go-ahead to pursue the necessary steps to develop the resort on the land at the top of the cliffs, in exchange for the green field site on the outskirts of the town.

The community protest group convened on Thursday evening.

"What now?" one member asked. "Council didn't pay any attention to community opposition. What avenues of appeal are available to us?"

All eyes turned to Alyssa. "This result is not unexpected. It was driven by financial considerations rather than environmental and community concerns. The next step, provided you are still unified in your opposition, is to lodge an appeal with Environment, Resources and Development Court. There will be fees to pay and a heap of paperwork to lodge as well, justifying our appeal." She looked around at them all. "If you're serious about opposing the project, lodging the appeal will be the start of a real bun fight. It will also need some community fund-raising."

Heated discussion followed, debating the pros and cons of any action, plus concern about the costs and any personal liability. As the meeting was held in the lounge bar of the Regal Hotel, a few beverages helped to lubricate the discussion and also encouraged some totally irrelevant comments, much to Alyssa's irritation. By the end of their meeting, they reached a consensus of sorts. Alyssa would drive up to Adelaide to consult with a contact from her old firm. Peter Tindale had extensive experience in submitting to and appearing before the ERD Court, and she would seek his advice on the strength of their position. That advice would be used in making their final decision and committing funds to the campaign.

"Let me make a quick phone call," Alyssa said. "If Peter is available tomorrow afternoon, I'll leave work early and catch him before he finishes for the day. He usually works late, and if he knows I'm coming, and I promise to shout him an after-work drink, he might hang around for me."

Peter sounded delighted to hear from her, and readily agreed to her request. "What else am I going to do late on a Friday afternoon?" he boomed down the phone. It reminded her of the hand that suddenly appeared on her knee at another after-work function, but she would know to keep the table between them this time. His expertise was too important to not meet him. She could then stay in Adelaide over the weekend, and perhaps catch up with Charlotte. Her townhouse hadn't sold yet, but her furniture was in storage, so she couldn't stay there. She would treat herself to a city hotel instead.

Paul shrugged when she told him she wanted to leave early. "Unless you have appointments, it's up to you how you manage your time. Tindale should give you good advice. See you next Monday."

Alyssa had mixed feelings driving back to the city. She had been away long enough that she had learned to appreciate the laidback lifestyle of a small coastal town, but… she had made the decision she would return. To that end, she would ask Peter to keep her in mind if he heard of any job opportunities. She couldn't help noticing though the increased level of traffic the closer she got to the city centre. City life would require some re-adjustment.

Peter was helpful. He listened attentively as she outlined the history of the project, and took note of the technical issues, such as the relevant zoning, proximity to the town centre, and any relatable precedents.

"It's important to understand that this is a long way from a done deal," he explained. "The clifftop land is zoned Community Land, and there is a process to be followed in revoking that, including commencing community consultation. You've still got time up your sleeve to canvass against this step in the process, before taking up the fight in court against the actual development proposal."

He hunched over his keyboard and peered intently at his computer screen. "I checked on precedents earlier today, and this isn't an isolated case. There was a similar incident down in the south east, where it was proposed that community land be exchanged with the local golf club. The local first nation's people strongly opposed that proposal as being culturally insensitive. Have you followed that line of investigation?"

They discussed the issues for the best part of an hour, before Alyssa shut down her laptop. "I think I have all the information I need for now. I was aware in general terms of the legislative processes, but you've clarified some of the issues for me. Thank you for that." She stood up. "I promised you a drink. Do you still go to the Bauhinia Bar on a Friday night?"

"Is the Pope a Catholic? Of course, I do."

They were almost the last to leave the office. A couple of diehards were still at their desks, but as Alyssa recalled, that was life for a city-based commercial lawyer. They strolled the short distance down the road to the bar that was a popular watering hole for the legal fraternity. The streets were busy with pre-Christmas activity, and shopfronts were decorated with coloured lights and festive displays. The city buzzed with anticipation, and when they arrived at the bar, it was packed with end-of-year revelers. Some had clearly kicked on from office Christmas parties; others were simply making the most of the vibe.

Alyssa ordered them a negroni each, and they joined a group of people she knew from her previous job. She should have anticipated who else might be there. Suddenly a hand slid around her waist, and a kiss was planted on her cheek.

"Hey, babe… you should have let me know you were coming."

Phillip. She looked around but he was on his own. No sign of the woman he'd cheated with, but if Charlotte was correct, that relationship had fizzled quickly. He nodded a greeting to other people in the group before turning his attention back to her.

She pushed her hair back off her face. "This is an impromptu trip. I needed to consult Peter on some matters relating to the ERD Court."

"You've asked the right person. This, I assume, is in relation to the development that you're opposing?"

"Yes. Council have voted to agree to the land swap, subject to community consultation. That only happened this week, so I'm on a fact-finding mission before the protest group decides on future action."

"Sounds a good idea. I'm just about to get myself a drink. Can I get one for anyone else while I'm at the bar? Alyssa? Peter?"

He obviously intended to join them. There was no reason why not. He knew everyone else present. He returned after a few minutes clutching a schooner of ale, and positioned himself next to Alyssa.

"Are you here for the weekend? Where are you staying?"

"At the Mercure Hotel in Hindmarsh Square. It's central and I can walk everywhere I need to go."

He nodded in response, but didn't push the conversation any further, instead engaging in conversation with some of the others. When Peter finally looked at his watch and declared it was time for him to make tracks, the ranks of those in the group had thinned. Phillip turned his attention back to Alyssa.

"Do you have any plans for dinner? There's a new Japanese restaurant that's opened near here. I've been meaning to try it for a while."

Alyssa quickly reviewed her options. She could get some take-away and take it back to her hotel room, but it seemed a shame not to make the most of city opportunities, now that she was here, and she did like Japanese food. It felt strange to be in Phillip's company again in the city. She noticed a few curious looks in their direction, and no doubt the gossip mill would fire up behind their backs. Phillip had been on his best behaviour on his recent visit to Sandy Bay, so she couldn't think of a valid reason why she shouldn't go with him.

"Sure. I'm always up for good Japanese food, and I'm not likely to get any in the Bay."

Phillip cast around inclusively at the others in their party. "Anyone else like to join us?"

The refusals were polite. Had to get home, had other obligations, etcetera, but Alyssa knew they would have refused to join them if they were starving and had nothing else to do. None of them would intrude. She brushed aside the uncomfortable feeling that they were making assumptions about her and Phillip.

He rang and reserved a table, allowing them thirty minutes to finish their drinks and stroll the short distance to the restaurant. Phillip courteously walked on the road side of the footpath. A couple of times, their hands brushed as they walked, reinforcing her awareness of their proximity. It reminded her of previous Friday nights, when they often explored new eating establishments after work, or patronized old favourites.

The restaurant was good, and so was Phillip's company. They slipped into the easy camaraderie based on having a shared history and interests, without the tedium of small talk. After the meal, he insisted on walking her back to her hotel, turning towards her at the entrance and grasping her by the shoulders.

"I've enjoyed tonight. Thank you for your company."

He leaned forward and gently deposited a kiss on her lips. He remained holding her for a moment, smiling and maintaining eye contact.

"Sleep tight, Allie. I'll call you tomorrow. There's a new exhibition at the art gallery you might like to see."

Releasing her, he turned and strode off up the street, leaving her in turmoil. He was the only person who called her Allie. He had awakened an intimacy she'd fought so hard to suppress. She wandered back to her room, and sat out on the balcony for a while, looking out over the lights of the city. She loved the sea views of Sandy Bay, but the city lights had an attraction of their own as well. The vibrancy beckoned her. It wasn't only the lights that played on her mind. The life she'd left behind also featured predominantly in her thoughts.

***

Saturday morning at the Central Market had been a long-standing ritual before she left the city. Alyssa wandered down early the next morning, ordering breakfast at Lucia's café and then cruising past the stalls she used to frequent. She stocked up on a range of goods she couldn't access in Sandy Bay, exchanging greetings with some of the stall-holders as she went. She finished up at the local bookstore, browsing the latest releases before hauling her purchases back to the hotel.

She had just finished putting the perishables into the fridge in her room when Phillip rang.

"Morning. Let me guess—you've been to the Market."

"Am I that predictable?"

"Yep. I mentioned the exhibition at the art gallery yesterday. Would you like to go? You can see the details online. It's a retrospective exhibition of Jeffrey Smart's work. I know you've always liked his art."

"Absolutely. I can't leave the city without seeing that. Give me a time and I'll meet you at the front of the gallery."

She met him on the steps of the gallery a bit before lunchtime. They strolled through the exhibition, taking their time and discussing each painting, what appealed about it and what they considered to be its strengths. That done, they stopped off at the gallery bistro for a light lunch, and then meandered through other halls within the gallery, revisiting paintings familiar from previous visits. On the way out, they browsed in the gallery shop, and Phillip purchased and presented to her a souvenir book featuring Jeffrey Smart's work.

Alyssa flipped through the pages with delight. "Phillip, you didn't have to do that."

"I know, but I wanted to. I know you'll appreciate it. He's a local boy made good really, as he was born and grew up in Adelaide."

"Thank you, I really appreciate it. I'll enjoy revisiting the paintings through its pages."

They wandered down North Terrace, past the museum and the state library. A mixture of tourists and locals were patronizing each of the facilities, or taking photos of the war memorial. Alyssa felt like a tourist in her own city, looking at the boulevard as many others were doing for the first time.

"I've enjoyed seeing you again," Phillip said. "I wanted to see that exhibition and probably would have but I much prefer seeing it with you. Alyssa, can we talk about us? I've missed you. Do you think we can start again?"

She felt a stab of panic and took a breath before turning to face him. He guided her to a park bench on the secluded walk adjacent to Government House, and they sat down. The plane trees threw a dappled light over the scene, but sunshine still illuminated his face. His eyes searched her face as she struggled to find the right answer. How could she reply when she no longer knew what the right answer was.

"Phillip, you hurt me so much with what you did. How do I know you won't do it again? How do I know you're sincere about wanting me, and not just the benefits that a relationship with me would bring?"

He looked puzzled at that, but didn't know what Charlotte had told her. "I know I hurt you and I'm desperately sorry about that. I've had a lot of time to think over my actions, and I know what you meant to me and continue to mean. We'd each become too caught up with our jobs and then neglected our relationship. If we get back together, I want it to be different; I want us to be different."

"How different?"

"We could set boundaries… not bringing so much work home, maintaining dedicated time for us… communicating honestly. If you think it would help, I'd be willing to try counselling."

She would have been stupid not to be aware that Phillip had been on his best behaviour, and was trying to get into her good books again, but still hadn't expected this conversation. On the plus side, she had enjoyed his company again without the sniping and bitching that had existed in the past. Who else would have known of her passion for Jeffrey Smart and ensured she got to see the exhibition?

On the minus side, did a leopard ever really change its spots? She had made a decision to sell the house and her time in Sandy Bay had made her realise that her life had become stale and it was time to carve a new path for herself. She enjoyed the more laid-back pace of life of recent months, and she'd made new friends. Okay, there was one friend, a tall man with mesmerizing green eyes, an unruly mop of hair and a total disregard for the pressures of city life. She cast that mental image aside. It was not him she had to think about right now... or was it?

"Phillip, I—"

"Don't say anything now. Promise me you'll consider it. I don't want to push you into an immediate decision."

"I was going to say, I need time to think about this."

He stretched his arm along the back of the bench, encompassing her shoulders. "It's Christmas soon. Neither of us should spend it alone. We could make this a Christmas to remember, and after that, who knows. We could at least talk about the future... us, perhaps some travel, children... We were going to get married."

Her head spun. Marriage! Children! She jumped up from the seat. "There are a lot of things we were going to do, but things have changed... I've changed."

"And I've changed, and surely that's for the better. Christmas together… that's all I ask for now. After that, we'll see. I don't want to rush this."

Alyssa breathed out and pushed the hair from her eyes. "I'm meeting Charlotte tonight, and I think before then, I need to go back to the hotel and rest."

Phillip stood up as well.

"No, don't come with me," Alyssa said. "I have a lot of thinking to do, and I'll do that better alone. I'll call you in a couple of days and let you know what I'm doing." She took a step back to keep herself out of arm's reach. She did not want him to kiss her. She did not want any pressure that might influence her thinking. "Thank you for inviting me to the gallery. I would be sorry to have missed it." Her words sounded oddly formal, but she needed to maintain her distance.

"I'll call you," she said again, and clutching her book to her chest, turned and walked back the way they'd come. She felt his eyes on her, but refused to look back. She didn't dare say anything to Charlotte about the conversation. She knew what her friend would say. Run, girl, as fast as you can. Could she really run from her past, or was her past part of her future? She had a couple of days to decide. Christmas was only a week away.

17 – The Orange-bellied Parrot

THE DRIVE BACK to Sandy Bay on the Sunday afternoon didn't take long. Tourists and day trippers were all travelling in the opposite direction, returning to the city so traffic flowed smoothly. If anything, she would have welcomed a longer journey as that might give her more think time.

Dinner with Charlotte the previous evening had been full of girl talk, laughter, and sparkling wine. It was great to relax and catch up on local gossip. Phillip did not enter the conversation, except in a very general sense. Alyssa knew that if Charlotte thought she was contemplating taking Phillip back, her friend would call her a fucking idiot. Charlotte was not one to mince words, and this was a decision that couldn't be coloured by her views.

She had expected to be relieved to be driving away from the city and returning to Sandy Bay, but Phillip had left her totally confused. They'd been together for so long. He knew her as well as her own family. Who else would have suggested the visit to the Gallery? He'd been on his very best behaviour on the last two occasions she'd seen him, first over the weekend in Sandy Bay, and now during this last weekend in Adelaide. Could she trust that he wouldn't stray again though? Was it really her fault that he did? He hadn't taken ownership of that indiscretion.

Tiger refused to talk to her when she arrived home. She'd arranged for a neighbour to feed him, and he evidently didn't approve. He stalked away from her as she carried her overnight bag up the stairs to the front door and then sat with his back to her.

"Honestly, Tiger, you're just as petulant as every other bloke I know. I thought you were above such behaviour."

The cat swished his tail, and the twitch of his ears indicated he knew she was talking to him. He even refused to eat until she walked away from his bowl, pretending that he wasn't hungry at all.

"Suit yourself. You don't have to sleep on my bed tonight. You can make yourself comfortable on the lounge."

Of course, when she woke up the next morning, he was curled up next to her and behaved as though nothing was wrong.

"I'm wise to you, Tiger. You just play with my emotions until you get your own way." The irony of it wasn't lost on her.

A new client had come into the office late on the Friday after she'd left for Adelaide, and Paul dumped the file on her desk. She hit the ground running, once she had her morning coffee in hand and was so engrossed in unravelling the complexities of the matter that she nearly didn't answer her phone when it rang. A glance at the screen told her that Max was calling. He didn't usually call her at work. Correction, he didn't usually call her at all.

She tapped <save> on her keyboard and answered the call. "Max, hi."

"You sound distracted. Is this a bad time to call? I'll be quick."

"No, that's okay," she lied. "I was deeply focused on a complex matter."

She heard him clear his throat. "I have some news you might like sooner rather than later. You know I set up the movement activated cameras, and there was nothing captured of interest. A few lizards and night birds, but nothing of consequence in relation to my assessment."

This was not news. Alyssa glanced at her watch, and peered into her coffee cup in the futile hope that some dregs remained.

"The thing is, something *has* turned up. To be specific, an orange-bellied parrot has arrived."

Alyssa resisted the urge to start doodling on her scratch pad. "What do you mean, it's arrived? Where has it been?"

"It's an endangered bird, normally domiciled in Tasmania, but migrates to the southern coast of the mainland for a few months each year. Its natural habitats are endangered, due to rising sea levels, coastal erosion and clearing of native vegetation. Some of that vegetation is in the headland area, and the bird depends on it."

Alyssa dropped her pen and sat up straighter. "So, what now?"

"I'll provide an addendum to my report, and will also notify the Department for Environment. I have the video evidence. The bird was at the little waterhole you showed me."

"Will it prevent the resort project from gaining development approval?"

"That's not my decision, but it's highly likely that the Council won't continue with the land swap and on that basis, the resort won't proceed, not in that location at least."

"That's fabulous news. The others will be thrilled when I let them know. I think you've saved the day."

"Just doing my job."

He sounded pleased with himself, and rightly so. She had never been one to deny a mistake when she'd made one. "I know I gave you a hard time when we first met. I made a lot of assumptions that weren't justified. I apologise for that."

"Forget it. I already have. You could make up for it though by having dinner with me tomorrow night at the *Saucy Fish*. Jeremy is staying with his grandparents and I'll have a child-free night."

"I'd like that. It will make a change from supper on the deck with Tiger."

Max laughed. "I'll pick you up at seven. See you then."

Alyssa sat for a while after disconnecting the call. She hadn't expected that news. What surprised her most was the relief she felt. Preserving the headland had been an obligation. She didn't resent that, but it influenced how she related to the town and enjoyed her time there. Now she could sit back and relax, perhaps join a walking group, or do more day trips around the region. With that thought in mind, she reached for her phone. There were people to notify.

***

Was this a date? Alyssa stood in front of her wardrobe, deciding what to wear. She'd only brought the basics with her. The rest of her wardrobe was packed in storage. She hadn't seen the need for glamorous evening wear, or cocktail outfits. Not that either would be appropriate for a meal at a waterfront restaurant in Sandy Bay. She settled on a simple jersey dress in deep navy with a scooped neckline and a skirt that flowed nicely. It was comfortable and forgiving.

Max picked her up exactly on time. Punctuality was sexy in a man. It showed respect and attention to detail. She'd kept an eye out for him, and when his car pulled into the driveway, she only had to grab her bag before coming down the stairs.

He jumped out the car, and coming around to the passenger side, opened the car door for her. As she slid past him into the seat, she smelt a mixture of soap and a light woody fragrance. Increasingly, it did feel like a date.

Max had booked a table on the deck, overlooking the water. The intense heat of the day had settled, and if they were lucky, they would get a frontline seat to a fabulous sunset in the next hour.

"I haven't been here for so long," Max commented. "My dining out excursions have been more kid-related in the last couple of years. From memory, they used to have a great salt-and-pepper flounder."

"I had lunch here recently with Delia Kennett. I'm sure you won't be disappointed."

This was also where she'd first met Emma, but Alyssa kept that detail to herself. The waiter appeared with the menus and took their drink orders, so conversation slowed while they considered their options. The waiter returned with a bottle of chilled Sauvignon Blanc, and poured them each a glass before placing the bottle in an ice bucket.

"Here's to the orange-bellied parrot," Alyssa said, raising her glass. I'm keen to make the acquaintance of our feathered friend. He's achieved what the rest of us might not have been able, not without a lot of effort and some money to boot."

Max clinked his glass against hers. "I can show you the video. I should have thought to download it to my phone. I've left the cameras in position, so I should collect further data. It's relevant, not just in this situation, but also for ornithologists who are studying the life-cycle of the parrot."

Local birds of the seagull variety were making themselves at home at the water's edge. They stood in the shallows, calling to each other and occasionally rising in the air in a raucous cloud before settling again. A small child ran shrieking among them, causing a flurried scattering, before they settled in front of a family party on the beach, waiting for any spare chips or other morsels.

This relaxed atmosphere was as far from the formal Japanese restaurant in the city as it was possible to get. The sea breeze carried with it a combined scent of brine and seaweed, but not offensively so. The scene took on a golden glow under the rays of the setting sun, and Alyssa noted that Max's normally tanned complexion assumed a peachy hue. His well-formed lips were similarly bathed, reminding her of the previous week when she'd kissed them. She tried not to compare her time spent with Max to the time spent with Phillip. They were such different men.

He noticed her staring and she quickly dropped her eyes, but not before noticing the slight smile that tugged at his lips and then disappeared. Their chosen meals arrived promptly, and that diverted his attention. They chatted about local issues, but skirted around anything personal. At the back of her mind was Phillip's request. She still hadn't given him an answer and had no idea what it should be.

"How is your meal?" Max interrupted her thoughts. "You looked to be miles away. I hope it meets your expectations."

She took a sip of her wine and opened her eyes wide to indicate that she was definitely alert. "Absolutely. I've not eaten here often, but it's always been first class. I was just lost in the ambience of the evening."

He glanced around at the views beyond the deck. "It's times like this I really appreciate where I live. The weather's great, the view is spectacular, the food is good and the company is even better. Why would you want to live anywhere else?"

She smiled weakly in acknowledgement, but didn't answer. It was a rhetorical question.

The sun had set by the time they finished their meal, leaving a deep blue sky in its wake. Soon it would be truly dark, but for now, there was enough ambient light on the beach.

"Shall we walk along the beach?" Max asked. "The tide won't be in for a while yet."

"Sure." Alyssa slipped her shoes off and walked through the cool sand. It felt natural when Max reached out and took her other hand. His hand was larger than hers, and his grip was firm without being restrictive. They strolled at the water's edge, allowing small wavelets to rush forth and swirl around their toes. Early moonlight danced over the waves, making them shimmer and glimmer.

"You know there is still some way to go before the development issues are fully resolved," Max began hesitantly. "Can we not let those issues come between us?"

She looked at him, trying to read his expression in the reduced light. "I know we didn't get off to a good start, but you were just doing your job. In spite of that, I do enjoy your company, and Jeremy is a great kid. He's a credit to you."

"I nearly forgot," Max said. "Jeremy reminded me to ask you again about Christmas."

She hoped the dim light covered the blush she could feel surging over her cheeks. "I'll let both of you know very soon, I promise."

Max stopped and pulled Alyssa around to face him. "I should also make clear that I'm not looking for a replacement mother for Jeremy. I haven't been *looking* for anyone but I have enjoyed being with you. I didn't expect to, but I do."

"Am I that difficult to like?"

"That's what I get for taking a lawyer to dinner! I didn't say that at all. Okay, you did get me offside in the beginning, and I thought you were a tad obnoxious, but aside from that, I've enjoyed our interaction... of all kinds," he added meaningfully.

As though to emphasize his meaning, he ran a finger over her lips before dropping a light kiss on them. "I like the idea of a relationship developing organically. Can we just see where this takes us?"

"Sure." Alyssa resumed walking, tugging him along with her. That way she didn't have to look directly at him. "Since we're being open here, I should say that I haven't come to Sandy Bay looking for a relationship either. Just the opposite. The offer of the job with Paul came at a time when my godmother needed a house-sitter, and I needed a break from city life."

She didn't want to mention that she ran away from a relationship with a cheating partner, a partner who now was pressuring her to give him a second chance. She could feel Max looking at her speculatively as he digested this information, but steadfastly looked straight ahead.

"Looks like slow and steady suits us both then," was the only comment he made.

❦

Max pulled up in the driveway of Seaclusion and applied the handbrake. "I've enjoyed this evening. I love my son dearly, but having some child-free adult time is appreciated.'

Alyssa unclipped her seatbelt. "It doesn't have to end so soon. Would you like to come in for coffee? I can't promise any Drambuie, but there might be something equally as appealing in the liquor cabinet."

"If you'd told me earlier, I would have brought some," he joked, "but yes, coffee would be good."

Is more on offer? Hell, it's so long since I've been in this situation, I'm no longer sure of dating etiquette.

He followed her up the stairs to the front of the house. The security light came on, and he stood to one side as she fumbled with the key and unlocked the door. Alyssa swung the door open and kicked off her shoes, wriggling her toes on the carpet.

"I've probably dropped sand everywhere now. I'll clean it up in the morning. Come and look at the view from the deck."

She led him outside again, and they leaned against the railing looking out over the headland, the cliffs and the sea beyond. "It's different to your view, but they're both spectacular."

He wrapped an arm around her shoulder, noting the sea breeze that had now sprung up. She stood about ten centimetres shorter than him, and he could smell the scent of her shampoo in her hair. He tried to focus on the view beyond the balustrade rather than the warm body leaning against him. It was now fully dark, and the sea surged in the distance like an alien force that could swallow anyone who came within reach.

The ocean had been his solace when Clara died but he had never lost his respect for the way it could play with and torment those who didn't abide by its rules. At the same time, the water could throw up amazing treasures. He wondered if that was happening now.

"Come inside while I make that coffee," Alyssa said. "I know all the barista tricks. Comes from city living and chatting up every barista within walking distance. What's your preference?"

She dragged out the coffee cups from a cupboard, as well as the coffee plunger. While the water was boiling, she also opened the liquor cabinet and after squinting into the inner recesses, pulled out a bottle of Frangelico.

"I'm sure Mary won't mind us sampling this. It's for a good cause. The alcohol should counteract the caffeine in the coffee. They go well together. If you like, I'll do a liqueur coffee with a dash of cream."

"Sounds good to me." While Alyssa busied herself with their drinks, he perused the book titles on the shelves in the lounge room and looked at the framed photos. She featured in a couple, one as a child with her godmother, and the other in a graduation photo. "Cute kid," he said as she carefully carried in the coffees and set them on the occasional table. She actually blushed, and that was cute too. "I reckon she stayed that way."

Alyssa bristled. "That makes me sound like a kewpie doll." She picked up her own coffee and took a sip, with the cream leaving a while moustache on her upper lip. If he'd had his phone handy, he would have taken a photo. Instead, he reached for a tissue from the box sitting on the sideboard.

"Allow me," he said as he took the mug from her hand and put it down on the table. She looked confused as he crumpled up the tissue, and then wiped off the cream. "A moustache isn't quite the look for a high-powered lawyer about town. I was tempted to kiss it off."

"Perhaps you should have."

Now she tells me. "Forgive me, I'm out of practice and a little slow on the uptake. I feel I've been negligent."

He reached over and drew her close. Her face lifted to his in anticipation, her eyes fixed on his almost in a challenge. He slid his hand down to the small of her back, pressing her body against his as he nibbled at her lips, gently at first and then with hunger and urgency. Her pace of breathing increased and he felt her breasts pressing against his chest. One of her hands wound itself around his neck and the other popped open the upper button of his shirt and slid over his skin. A tide of exquisite longing swept over him. Her dress clung to her body, and he felt the outline of her taut buttocks beneath his hand. He'd fantasized about doing that.

She pulled away enough to allow her to look up at him. "You don't have to go home tonight? I'm not meaning to be forward, but if you want to take this somewhere more comfortable, I wouldn't object."

"I love forward women. If that's an invitation, then I accept." Even if he hadn't spoken, a straining portion of his anatomy would have given the game away.

Alyssa seized his hand and began to lead him towards the passage leading to other rooms in the house. He was about to ask whether he should bring their coffees, when her mobile rang from the depths of her bag, earlier slung on the kitchen bench. She looked startled.

"Who would that be at his time of night? Perhaps it's Mary. I'd better check."

While she rummaged in her bag, Max took a mouthful of his own coffee, being careful to wipe his mouth on the back of his hand. It tasted good. He made a mental note to buy a bottle of Frangelico for future occasions. He turned his back on Alyssa, but heard her flip open her phone and answer the call. She spoke softly, but he could still make out the conversation.

"Phillip? Do you know what time it is?... I'll let you know. I can't talk now... I'll call you tomorrow."

Phillip. The man from the farmer's market. She wasn't unencumbered after all. Whatever the situation, he had no wish to get embroiled in her intimate affairs. There was no point in staying longer. He picked up his car keys as she disconnected the call and dropped her phone back into her bag.

"Sorry, it will only complicate matters if I stay. I enjoyed this evening. I'll let myself out." Even to himself, he sounded stilted and distant. He registered the shocked look on her face as he crossed the room to the front door. She didn't say a word or try to stop him, just stood and stared.

As he reversed his car down the driveway, he glanced up at the deck and saw her standing there, watching him. She didn't wave.

18 – The Decision

ALYSSA WATCHED MAX drive away, unable to think straight about what had just happened. Up until then, it had been a perfect night. One minute, the passion level was rising between them, and the next the shutters came down. He must have heard her speaking to Phillip, but she hardly said anything. It only lasted a couple of minutes, if that. Why did that send him running?

On entering the lounge room again, she noticed the liqueur coffees still sitting on the small table. Neither of them had finished their drink. The mugs were still warm. She carried them to the kitchen, intending to rinse them out, but with a change of heart, took hers outside. Tiger followed her, as though knowing she needed company at this time. She sat in one chair and the cat curled up in another.

The driveway remained clear, except for her car parked at the top. A tiny irrational thought said that perhaps Max didn't really go, or that he'd had second thoughts and come back. He hadn't. Alyssa sipped her coffee, not caring if it left a moustache or not. She could lick it off. Her experiences with Max needed a debrief, though Tiger couldn't offer much constructive advice. At least he could listen.

Max had stirred sensual emotions she'd repressed ever since that afternoon she walked in on Phillip and the skank, as she still liked to think of the other woman. She missed the familiar comfort of the physical connection she'd enjoyed with Phillip. After so long together, their bodies spooned easily in bed, they knew each other's likes and patterns of behaviour. Dammit, they had fitted together so comfortably as a couple.

God, was that the problem? Had she become predictable and boring? Was that why Phillip strayed? Had it been her fault? No, that was irrational victim blaming, but a niggling question remained. Had her behaviour played a part in what happened? When that relationship had been snatched from her, she had shut down emotionally. She must have given the wrong signals and driven Max away.

"What do you think, Tiger? Am I destined to be a single woman with a houseful of cats?"

The cat opened his eyes and looked at her, but after a quiet stare, shut them again. Alyssa took the hint and after picking up her glass, returned inside. There were no obvious answers to her questions.

Normally, she wore light cotton sleeping shorts to bed, but this time she was naked when she slipped between the sheets. She wanted the cool sensation of the cotton fabric against her skin, getting in touch again with her body. Drinking coffee late at night hadn't been smart. Instead of drifting into sleep, she lay staring at the ceiling, with the events of the evening playing in an endless loop.

When she'd first met Phillip, she had been young, sexy, and on an upward trajectory at work. The attraction had been mutual, and she'd thought of him then as a kindred spirit, one who understood her world and where she was going in life. That belief had been sorely tested.

She had come to believe that she and Max were potentially compatible, but the last thing she wanted was make a fool of herself if the feelings were not reciprocated. She'd enjoyed her evening with him. Conversation had flowed freely, and the telltale signs of attraction had been there: direct eye contact, hands accidentally brushing against each other. Did he somehow sense that she was damaged goods? No longer young and sexy or on an upward trajectory? Perhaps she gave off subtle signals of which she was unaware. On the other hand, Phillip still wanted her. He hadn't expressly said that, but he wanted her to come back. First Christmas and then...?

She might have behaved too hastily in rushing off that day, quitting her job and putting the house on the market. It had been a gut reaction. Perhaps they should have tried counselling. That option hadn't crossed her mind at the time, but now it did. What would she say? Did she still love Phillip or was she just scared of losing that part of her life? The thoughts tumbled over themselves for more than an hour before she finally fell asleep.

Poor sleep left her with a disgruntled feeling the next morning. Remembering how abruptly Max had left didn't help either. Alyssa reviewed the previous night's ponderings. She didn't want to act hastily, but by the time she had fallen asleep, she'd reached a decision of sorts. She would spend Christmas in Adelaide with Phillip, but staying in a hotel again. That would allow her to retain a measure of control over their time together.

After vacating the townhouse, Phillip had taken an apartment in the city, and would probably be happy if she stayed there, but that didn't seem like a good idea. Staying with Charlotte was another option, but complicated. Charlotte would tell her she was insane to even consider taking Phillip back, and any decisions she made had to be without outside influence. A hotel was best.

The drive along the coastal road to the office in Port Reilly always provided a pleasant transition to her working day. Minimal traffic, sea views, and short drive. She pulled into the carpark at the same time as Paul, and they both wandered inside together, dumping their bags in their respective offices and then meeting up by the espresso machine in the kitchen.

"I hear you had a pleasant dinner at the Saucy Fish last night. Something happening with you and Max I should know about?"

Alyssa tried not to obviously roll her eyes. "Are there no secrets in this town? Max and I are just friends. Who told you, anyway?"

"Jacinta, and one of her friends who spotted you told her, and no… there are no secrets in this town." He grinned wickedly. "She'll be very disappointed at the *just friends* comment."

"We were celebrating the arrival of the orange-bellied parrot, that's all. Sorry to be such a disappointment."

She carried her coffee back to her office, keen to prevent further questioning. There was nothing to tell about her and Max. Friends it was, and Jacinta should be happy with that, given how their association had started. She didn't want to even think about Max. The evening had ended as an embarrassment. She'd all but thrown herself at him like a brazen floozy and then he'd fled. She wouldn't be telling Jacinta that juicy piece of information.

Although she told herself she'd made up her mind where she would spend Christmas, she still hesitated about calling Phillip. She placed her phone within arm's reach on the desk, and then sat staring out the window, as though she might find last-minute inspiration on the appropriate course of action. Pedestrians walked past the window, but none glanced in her direction. She was on her own.

She picked up the phone and dialed. He picked up almost immediately.

"Alyssa… sorry I rang so late last night. I remembered that you usually sat up late reading or working on files and thought you'd still be awake."

He was right. She did usually do that. His timing last night had been unfortunate, but she had no intention of telling him that. "Country life… you know, fresh air and all that. Old patterns change. Anyway, I was ringing to say I will come to Adelaide for Christmas. I'll drive up on the twenty fourth and stay at the Mercure again, if they have an available room. I'm not sure how long I'll stay; there are a few people I'd like to catch up with."

"You can stay with me, it's no trouble."

"I remember the bachelor pad you had when I first met. Your current flat is probably no better equipped. Besides, I'm just coming back for Christmas. It doesn't change anything else. I'm not ready to be pushed into anything."

His silence said more than he did. "Okay, but you will be here in time for Christmas Eve, won't you? Remember how we'd walk along the river each year, admiring the lights and then celebrating with cocktails at the Hyatt? I thought we could do that again."

"Sure. That sounds nice." It did, too. Christmas was all about familiarity and ritual and this was one they had always enjoyed. "I'll leave the office at lunchtime."

They made a few other arrangements before she disconnected the call and then made a booking at the hotel. They had a room and were pleased to welcome her back so soon. Arrangements were all in place. All that remained was to speak to Max. That could wait until that evening. She opened her laptop and logged on.

She didn't ring Max that day, nor the next. She told herself she was busy and didn't have time, but in reality, she wasn't sure what to say. *Sorry I came on strong. Sorry I scared you off, and by the way, tell Jeremy I won't be around on Christmas Day.* That wasn't right though. Max had kissed her too, and gave every indication that he not only enjoyed it but wanted to take things further.

Perhaps I had garlic breath? Why didn't I think to clean my teeth when we arrived home. Surely the liqueur coffee would have covered that up?

The safest option was not to mention the night of their dinner at all, and simply say that she would be in Adelaide over Christmas. She decided to call that evening, but opted to go down to the bay for a swim first.

With the long hot summer days, the water was almost lukewarm. She hadn't been swimming nearly enough, which was odd, given that she lived so close to the beach. Mostly she just walked along the sand or paddled. This time, she pulled on her swimming costume and plunged into the surf, initially rising up with each incoming swell before the foaming top formed and swamped her, but then plucking up the courage to dive underneath the breaking wave, surfacing after it had passed above her. The undercurrent tugged at her legs, pulling her sideways in the water. Easier to float, watching the drifting clouds and the odd seagull circling above.

By the time she emerged from the sea with water streaming down her body, she felt thoroughly pummeled. Her hair was plastered to her face, and she swept it back with one hand while tugging the leg of her swimsuit down with the other. The costume had ridden up while she was in the water.

"Hey Dad, there's Alyssa!"

She would know that voice anywhere. Where was her towel? Max and Jeremy stood in front of her, one of them obviously pleased to see her and the other? His expression was not so easy to interpret. Alyssa was conscious that her wet costume left little to the imagination. Okay, they were on a beach and there were plenty of skimpier outfits than hers, but when Max turned those steady eyes on her, she felt exposed and virtually naked. She reached for her towel, lying on the sand a few steps away, and wrapped it around herself, sarong style. She felt under-dressed beneath his gaze.

Max nodded a greeting. "Good day for a swim." He sounded polite but almost formal.

"It's been a busy couple of days; I needed some exercise after sitting most of the day." She swallowed, wanting to make a quick getaway but not appearing to do so. "This time of year is always a bit manic. Everyone wants everything done by Christmas."

"We're going to look at Christmas lights later," said Jeremy. "We have to wait until it gets dark to see them properly. Dad's letting me stay up later tonight."

"And so he should. Christmas lights are worth staying up late for."

"And we've decorated the tree." The child paused and looked at her hopefully. "Are you coming for Christmas? You could see the tree then."

She slid a look at Max before answering. His head was tilted to one side, giving the impression he was waiting for the answer too, but he didn't say anything. "Sorry, Jeremy. It turns out I won't be able to come. I have to drive up to the city for Christmas, but I can slip around tomorrow evening and inspect the tree if that's convenient to you and your dad."

Jeremy looked crestfallen, but peered up at his father. "Is it? Can Alyssa come and see the tree?"

"Sure, if that fits with her schedule."

"It does. I wouldn't have offered otherwise." She shivered. "This wind is turning cold. I'd better grab my gear and get back to the cottage. Tiger will be waiting for his dinner." She picked up her duffle bag from where she'd left it on the sand. "See you tomorrow evening."

Max watched her labored progress through the loose sand towards the steps that led up the cliff face. He hated to see Jeremy disappointed, but better it happened now than later. Christmas was a time when the boy keenly felt the loss of his mother, even though his memories were hazy and linked to photos in their albums rather than the warm and loving woman. There was no way he could let Alyssa or any other woman get Jeremy's hopes up of a typical family Christmas, when she was marking time until returning to the city. Returning to Phillip more like.

He told himself that his disappointment was all on Jeremy's behalf. He had enjoyed her company, but never expected anything to develop between them. It had been dinner and some flirtatious behavior, that was all. Maybe there had been a slim possibility for something closer to develop between them, but it rankled that he was wrong. He would develop better defenses in future.

Now that the project was unlikely to proceed, she wouldn't need to liaise with him anymore. Still, perhaps he would get some of that Frangelico. You never knew when the need for a liqueur coffee might arise.

19 – Christmas Drinks

SHE COULDN'T GO empty handed. What did one give a six-year-old boy? She searched the aisles of the local toy shop and settled on the traditional fallback—a Lego spaceship kit. It had enough pieces that he would be kept busy for hours. With that purchase made, she thought she should get something for Max too but she didn't know him that well. What did he enjoy? He already had Delia's book. As she passed the local bottle shop, the solution jumped out at her. A bottle of Frangelico.

A text message exchange during the day established that seven would be a good time to visit that evening. The lights would be shining on the tree, and there would be some time before Jeremy had to be in bed. She carefully wrapped the two presents, along with others intended for Adelaide recipients. While she filled in time before leaving, she also laid out her suitcase on the bed and started packing that. The following day was Christmas Eve, and in keeping with her plans, she would be leaving work early.

As she made the short drive to Max's house, she noted the array of lights festooning the streets. Some people went to extremes, complete with an illuminated Santa and sleigh riding across the roof, then others had nothing at all. A Christmas wreath hung on Max's front door, and a brightly-lit star was suspended in a window. She pressed the doorbell, and heard small feet thudding towards her on the other side of the door.

"She's here!"

The door swung open to reveal Jeremy's face lit up with excitement. "Do you know it's only two days until Christmas? Dad says the weather should be fine, so Santa won't have trouble finding us. He has a long way to come, because we're in the southern hemisphere and he lives at the North Pole."

"He probably uses GPS," she replied gravely. "That way, even if the skies are cloudy, he'll still find his way."

"I'll tell my dad that."

This was said with obvious relief. Max had entered the hall behind him, and indicated that his son should stand aside and let her in. He must have heard her comment about the GPS, as he gave her an amused side-eye.

"Lucky that Santa is technically savvy."

The tree had been erected in the lounge room. Max had found a real tree somewhere, as evidenced by the scattering of pine needles around the base. Alyssa inhaled deeply. It even smelled like a pine tree. She had an instant flashback to childhood Christmases, when her father always found a real tree. After her parents split, her mother reverted to a synthetic tree, which was dismantled and stored in the attic by New Year's Day.

Jeremy took her by the hand and lead her towards the tree. "Dad put it in the pot and then we decorated it together. He put the lights on it though. We made some of the decorations. Do you like it?"

She was aware of Max hovering in the background, though he'd hardly spoken to her. She had the impression that he listened for her reply just as intently as his son. She noticed the multi-coloured pine cones and remembered painting similar decorations when she was a child. She also made paper chains, and garlands using foil milk bottle tops.

"It's the best tree I've seen this year. I've got a couple of presents as well that can go underneath. I'm not sure if you want to leave them until Christmas morning or if you want to open them now."

The boy glanced uncertainly at his father. "Dad?"

"I think we leave them until Christmas morning. You can ring Alyssa later to thank her."

"Okay."

He carefully placed both parcels under the tree, giving his present a little shake as he did. She and Max exchanged complicit smiles as they noticed the action. Who hadn't tried to guess the contents of presents before?

"Can I offer you a drink? Glass of wine, perhaps? Gin and tonic?"

She accepted his offer of the gin, and Jeremy scored a lemonade. They sat chatting in the lounge room until Max looked ostentatiously at his watch.

"Time for bed, mate."

"But it's not properly dark yet."

"That's because it's summer. You wake up much earlier as well, so bed."

Jeremy turned big eyes on Alyssa. "Will you read me a story?"

She looked at Max uncertainly. She didn't want to intrude. This must be a regular father-son bonding time.

He shrugged. "It seems I've been usurped. If you have the time… Only one story, okay?" The last comment was delivered to his son.

"Tell me when you've cleaned your teeth and got your pyjamas on, and I'll come down to your room."

Jeremy scampered off.

Max raised his glass to her. "Don't feel you have to do this. He's taking advantage of your good nature."

"I'm quite happy to read him a story. He's a sweet kid, and anyway… it's Christmas."

When Jeremy called out from his room, she went in and made herself comfortable on the bed. He'd already picked out a book, but wanted to chat for a while first.

"Does Santa come to your house too?"

"He focusses on all the houses where he knows there are kids living. He would get tired out if he had to reach all the adults as well."

"I s'pose. If you stayed here, though, he could come to you as well."

This conversation had the potential to stray into tricky territory. "He could, but I'm sure he'll find me in the city if he has time."

"I wish you were coming here for Christmas."

Don't do this to me, Jeremy! Making a decision was difficult enough as it was. "I'll see you when I get back, and you can tell me all about your Christmas then."

"Jeremy, don't pester Alyssa." She hadn't heard him come, but Max leant against the door frame, arms folded. He must have been listening to their conversation. "Did you pick out the story you wanted?"

Alyssa picked up the book which was lying on the bed, and opened it to the first page of the Muddle-Headed Wombat. "I'm good at finding things, but I'm good at losing things too…" she read. She noticed his eyes closing, and by the time she was four pages in, Jeremy was fast asleep. She closed the book and kissed him lightly on the forehead.

"Sleep tight, little man."

Max waited in the lounge room with fresh glasses of gin and tonic. "I listened to the first couple of pages, but I almost know that book off by heart. You have a pleasant reading voice, by the way." He handed her the drink. "I figured after all that reading, your throat might be a bit dry."

She massaged her throat. "It's not too bad, but I never say no to another G and T. It's such a great summer drink. It always says 'Christmas' to me."

"No doubt, you'll have a few in Adelaide, then."

"Yes… no… I mean, maybe. I don't have any firm plans in that regard."

"Sounds like most of your plans relate to not being here."

She lifted her chin a fraction. Was he giving her a hard time? "Max, I have things I need to do in Adelaide, people I need to—"

"Look, it's none of my business. You spend Christmas where you want and with whoever you want."

"It's just that I have unfinished business. Some things in life get complicated." *At least, they do in mine.*

"Like I say, you don't need to explain. Cheers." He raised his glass. "Here's to a very merry Christmas."

Alyssa didn't stay much longer. Jeremy was asleep and after all, he was the one who had invited her. She finished her drink and stood up, placing her glass on the occasional table. "Thank you for the G and T. I have some packing to do. I hope you both enjoy your Christmas. I'll be back sometime between Christmas and New Year."

"I appreciate you dropping in. You've made a small boy very happy."

He muttered something under his breath, which she didn't quite catch but it almost sounded like "Bad luck about the big boy".

He walked her to the car, standing to one side as she unlocked it and threw her bag across to the passenger seat. She turned to face him, still puzzling over the comment she may or may not have heard.

"Great tree, by the way."

His eyes didn't leave hers. Propping one hand against the side of the car, he reached out and cupping his other hand against the side of her face, leaned forward and gently kissed her, almost regretfully.

"And what about Sandy Bay, Alyssa? Do you have any unfinished business here?"

Very little work had been done in the office that morning. Jodie had festooned the reception area with tinsel and a miniature Christmas tree sat on the counter. Paul had drawn the line at Christmas carols being played on repeat throughout the office, for which Alyssa and probably their clients were sincerely grateful. Jodie had sighed, but an air of festive anticipation had permutated through the week, interspersed with an almost manic pressure to get work done before the summer break. The office always closed between Christmas and the new year, but this year Paul had decided they should take the first week of January off as well.

"We need a decent break. The phones will be diverted to an answering service, so if there are any emergencies, we'll still be contactable."

Jodie brought in some of Haig's handmade Christmas pudding truffles, and they nibbled on those with their early morning coffee.

"This is a decadent start to the day." Alyssa licked the chocolaty residue from her fingers. "They're so rich, I might not need any lunch."

Jodie's face dropped. "But we've got our Christmas lunch today. I've booked the table."

Jacinta was joining them, plus Meredith, Alyssa's predecessor who was on maternity leave.

"I'm sure I'll manage to eat something. I try to pace myself in the lead up to Christmas. Every year, I tell myself I won't overeat, but inevitably I spend January trying to lose the weight I put on with over-indulgence."

"Tell me about it." Jodie patted her belly. "It's started already. I could hardly do up my zip this morning."

Alyssa had a few calls to make and a property transfer document to lodge, but she'd pushed her deadlines to the previous day in anticipation of a non-productive work day. She had already packed. Her bag was sitting in the lounge room ready for her to grab and go after the lunch. A neighbour had agreed to feed Tiger and water the garden. Alyssa would search for suitable treats from the Central Market in Adelaide to bring back as a thank-you gift.

Raucous chatter bounced off the walls in the restaurant making people strain to hear each other. Diners wore paper hats at some of the tables and read out the corny jokes found inside their Christmas crackers. Alyssa was relieved that they neither wore the hats, not pulled the crackers at their table. That level of public exuberance didn't sit comfortably with her.

Jacinta grabbed a chair next to her. "So… your first Christmas in Sandy Bay. You must be starting to feel like a local."

"Not quite my first Christmas. I spent a few here as a kid with my parents and Mary." She sipped her drink, non-alcoholic in consideration of the drive to the city later that afternoon, and the inevitable booze buses that would be out in force. Being done for DUI was not a good look for a solicitor.

"Anyway, I'm not spending Christmas here. I'm driving back to Adelaide this afternoon. I'll be there for a few days."

"So, you and Max…?" Jacinta trailed off, her voice reflecting disappointment but her raised eyebrows asking the question.

"There's no 'me and Max'. We're friends, that's all. *Keep saying that. You might convince yourself.*

"That's a pity. You seemed well-suited, and you're both single." A suspicious look crossed Jacinta's face. "You still are, aren't you? You haven't met anyone else since leaving that dropkick in Adelaide?"

Alyssa dropped her eyes. Was that how people thought of Phillip? To be fair, she'd probably used that word and worse when she'd first moved to Sandy Bay, but still…

"Actually, Phillip and I are on better terms these days." She tried not to sound defensive. "We were together for so long… we have a lot of shared history. I need to know if we can salvage anything from that."

"Oka-a-y" Jacinta didn't say any more, but she didn't need to. Her attitude said it for her. Later, as they all prepared to leave the restaurant, Jacinta gave her a big hug. "I hope you have a wonderful Christmas, and remember… the new year is all about looking forward, not looking back."

Alyssa checked the house once more and gave Tiger a pat before climbing into the car. The feeling of finally being on holidays lifted her spirits. It always put a lightness in her step, only this time she was driving away from Sandy Bay instead of towards it as she'd done in earlier years.

The receptionist at the Mercure welcomed her warmly. "Good to see you again, Ms. Finchley. I hope you enjoy your Christmas with us. If you're planning on dining in the restaurant for Christmas lunch, I advise you to make a reservation now. It's a popular day."

Alyssa thanked her and took her room key. She'd been upgraded to a premium suite on this stay, in recognition of her returning guest status. Once in her room, she drew back the curtains and surveyed the city skyline, splayed out below. The view stretched towards the river and the entertainment precinct. The spire of St Peter's Cathedral pierced the skyline in the distance, marking the division between the city proper, and the suburb of North Adelaide. This was an area of gracious stone mansions and terraces, established by the city's forefathers and commanding a hefty price if ever they came on the market. It was a far cry from the view at Sandy Bay.

She gave Charlotte a call to let her friend know she'd arrived. As Alyssa had known would be the case, Charlotte had called her a bloody idiot on learning of her intentions to spend Christmas with Phillip.

"For an intelligent woman, you can be incredibly stupid at times, but it's your life. You've got to mess it up in your own way."

That topic of conversation was then dropped, and they made arrangements instead for their own catch-up plans over the holiday break. Good female friends were worth their weight in gold.

"You've arrived already!" she screeched over the phone.

"A bit earlier than I expected. I had a clear run into the city. All the traffic was heading in the opposite direction."

"What are you doing now?"

"I'm meeting Phillip at six, but have no plans before that."

"Good. You can join us. You'll know everybody. There are a couple of people from the office and others from connections about town. We're having Christmas drinks at the Belgian Beer Café in the East End. See you soon."

Charlotte rang off. She presumably didn't consider that Alyssa might not fall in with this plan, but then she always had been bossy. Alyssa freshened her lipstick and slipped her wallet plus a small gift for Charlotte into a handbag and surveyed herself in the mirror. An aberrant strand of hair needed pushing back into place, but otherwise she was presentable.

The bar was teaming when she arrived, with a noise level to match. Alyssa pushed her way through the crowd and heard Charlotte before seeing her. Amazingly, there was still an empty chair at the table.

"I saved it for you," Charlotte stated triumphantly. "You didn't think I'd make you stand, did you? Jonathan, fetch the lady a drink. She'll have champagne."

Jonathan obediently rose and disappeared in the direction of the bar. The two women hugged, and inexplicably Alyssa felt her eyes begin to prickle with tears. It felt so good to hold her friend close, someone who knew her and with whom there was no pretense.

Looking around the group, she saw that Charlotte was right; she did know them all. In between the usual banter and tall stories focused on the legal profession, they caught up on personal news and industry gossip. Alyssa kept her eye on the time and paced her alcohol consumption. The rest of the evening still stretched before her.

She enjoyed the convivial company and chatter, but looking at her watch, knew she had to go. A visit to the ladies' powder room first would be smart, given the amount of both champagne and water that she'd drunk, but after that she would bid them farewell and slide out. She'd already placed the small gift into Charlotte's bag, but the two of them would catch up again in the next couple of days.

Standing groups of revelers filled the room, and she had to push around them as she made her way to the ladies'. That was when she saw him. Phillip sat in a booth in a corner of the room, and he wasn't alone. He sat close to a woman on the same bench seat, too close to be passed off as a Christmas drink with a colleague. Alyssa had only glimpsed the woman all those months ago, but she knew who it was. The woman she'd sprung in bed with Phillip.

She froze, unable to move either forward or back. Her stomach clenched and any moment she might be sick. As she stood frozen to the spot, Phillip looked at his watch. He said something to the woman and then leaned forward and kissed her. He picked up his phone. She knew what was happening. He was about to leave to keep his appointment with her.

That realization galvanized her into action. Turning, she shoved her way back through the crowd to where Charlotte sat.

"Sorry. Something has come up. I've got to go. I'm driving back to Sandy Bay."

20 – Unfinished Business

HOW COULD SHE have been so stupid? In her head, she heard Charlotte saying, *I told you so.* She had to pay for the first night's accommodation at the hotel, but that was a small price for the error in judgement. A range of popular expressions flashed through her mind as she drove.

'Once a cheater, always a cheater.'

'A leopard never changes its spots.'

Other times she just resorted to "You fucking bastard". Even yelled out loud, it didn't make her feel much better. She gripped the steering wheel so tightly the whites of her knuckles showed. She should have known better. Alyssa looked down at the dashboard and realized her speed had crept above the limit. She lifted her foot, not wanting to be done for speeding, especially after she had been drinking champagne.

She had no desire to speak to Phillip, ever again. When she returned to the hotel room to collect her luggage and check out, she had messaged him.

<Enjoy Christmas with the skank in the red dress. Don't contact me again.> Then she blocked his number, something she now wished she had done earlier.

Looks like it's going to be Christmas for one This is not what I signed up for. She had never previously spent Christmas on her own. Too late, she realized she could easily have stayed in Adelaide and spent those few days with Charlotte. Her friend would have welcomed her with open arms and a generous heart. She hadn't stopped to think. Her gut reaction had been to run. It would be Christmas in Sandy Bay after all. Her unfinished business was definitely done and dusted. She had no doubts about that now.

Night had set in when she arrived back in Sandy Bay. Strands of coloured lights strung across High Street created a festive atmosphere, and shop windows were alight with Christmas scenes or nativity layouts. Families wandered the main street, many clutching ice cream cones. The air of anticipation was apparent.

She kept driving and pulled up in the driveway of Seaclusion. Rather than climb out of the car, she sat considering her options. The thought kept running through her head that perhaps she had made the wrong choice. She'd chosen to address the wrong unfinished business. What would he say if she told him that… if she told Max her unfinished business lay in Sandy Bay after all?

There was only one way to find out. Starting the car again, Alyssa reversed out of the driveway and turned in the direction of Max's home. She had to do this now. If she stopped to think about it, she would chicken out. As it was, her heart was doing a tap dance in sheer terror.

On impulse, she stopped at the late-night supermarket and made a quick purchase before continuing her journey. She pulled up in the street outside Max's house. Lights were on inside, and Max's car was in the driveway, indicating he was home. She opted against parking behind his vehicle in case she needed to leave quickly.

Picking up her purchase, safe in a concealing bag, she knocked on the door. The outside security light had come on, placing her in the spotlight. Measured footsteps approached from the other side. Not Jeremy then. The door swung open and Max stood there, looking at her with a mixture of confusion and astonishment. He opened the door wider, inviting her in.

"I wasn't expecting you this evening. Jeremy's already in bed."

"I hoped he would be." She held out the bag. "I thought you might be in need these to leave out for the reindeer."

He peered into the bag and laughed. "Carrots? You've brought me a bag of carrots? We've put out some lemonade and a piece of cake for Santa, but forgot about the reindeer. I'll leave a few carrot tops around and tell him I thought about the reindeer after he went to bed."

He led her through to the kitchen. "Are you telling me you drove all the way back from Adelaide to give me a few carrots?"

"Not exactly, but sort of."

"I'm all ears."

"Do you think I could have a cup of tea?" She definitely didn't want any more alcohol, but her dry, parched throat screamed out for a drink. It also bought her a little time in which to gather her thoughts.

The calculated look he gave her indicated he saw through this ruse, but he obligingly filled the kettle and put a couple of mugs on the benchtop.

"I did go to Adelaide, with the intention of staying for Christmas and a few days beyond that, but not long after I arrived, I realized I'd stuffed up. I had thought I might have made a mistake in quitting my old life, but I've been reminded that I did so for a good reason."

Max dropped a tea-bag into each mug and fetched the milk from the fridge. "Would I be right in assuming that some aspects of your old life involved a man? Specifically, your breakfast companion of a couple of few weeks back?"

So, Max remembers Phillip. "Yes, they did. I haven't spoken about him before, because there was nothing to tell. Phillip and I were together for a long time. We worked in the same profession, were planning marriage and talking kids. He must have changed his mind, as I discovered him in a compromising situation with another woman."

She bit her lip. The story sounded embarrassingly tawdry. "As far as I was concerned when I came to Sandy Bay, he was locked in my past. I intended to forge a new life and there was nothing to tell. When he suggested that what we had was too good to turn my back on and that I should give him another chance, I wondered if he was right. I wanted to find out for sure, and I did. I was an idiot to be taken in by the bullshit."

"Strong words."

"With good reason." *Maybe I need a strong drink with that tea!* "I told you last night I had unfinished business to address, and today, I did that. It's definitely finished There was no point in my staying in the city, so I drove back to Sandy Bay."

Max carried the mugs over to the table and sat as well. "And the carrots?"

"That part is easy. I remembered that a small boy was keen for me to join you both for Christmas. The carrots are a peace offering. If the invitation still stands, I'd love to come."

He didn't answer straight away, leaving her with the uncomfortable feeling that he was about to retract the invitation. If that was the case, she should leave now.

"Look, keep the carrots. I shouldn't have bothered you. You probably have a few things to do this evening, so I'll get out of your hair." She reached for her car keys.

"Do you always jump to conclusions as quickly as this? On reflection, silly question. Of course, you do. Firstly, you will make a small boy very happy. He'll be thrilled when I tell him. For what it's worth, I'll be happy as well. Secondly..." He paused. "... secondly, I'm glad you sorted out your unfinished business and can put that behind you. It means that you can move on with your life."

She left her car keys where they were and reached for her mug of tea instead. "I intend to. I'm not absolutely sure what that will entail, but in part that is what's exciting. From here, I could do anything."

"Sure. Anything." Max nodded his agreement.

"Am I interrupting?" she asked. "Should you be feeding the reindeer or leaving footprints or whatever it is that Santa does? I don't believe my parents ever did that sort of thing for me, and I've not had any children of me own, so..."

"There are a few things, but it won't take long. First, I'll check that he's still asleep. He was so excited tonight, I thought he'd never drop off."

He crept down the hallway in bare feet, and eased Jeremy's bedroom door open. Moments later, he was back. "Out like a light. Santa leaves a sack of presents under the tree, and then there's the cake that needs to be eaten and the lemonade that needs to be drunk. I did suggest that perhaps Santa would like a beer, but Jeremy insisted that Santa wouldn't want beer while he was working."

"Smart kid. Have you got any icing sugar?"

"Probably. Why?"

"It's powdered snow. Santa's footprints show up more clearly. I read about it somewhere. Just be careful not to keep walking in it."

"You know more about this than you think. The cake and lemonade are on the coffee table by the tree. I'll get the icing sugar, and you can do what you need to do with the carrots."

The carrots still had leafy greens attached to the top. Alyssa took a couple and snapped them into pieces outside the front door. She added some toothmarks in the pieces that still have greenery attached, and requested that Max drop other bits in the compost bin.

"I'm not going to eat that much raw carrot at this time of night."

"Okay, but while I do that, you can sprinkle the snow. I've already dealt with the Santa food inside."

When he returned, he surveyed the scattered icing sugar, shaking his head. "You'll have to come back tomorrow. Someone's got to clean up this mess!"

"You've got to do the footsteps first. Careful not to tread in it and come outside."

Once he had maneuvered himself out the door, Alyssa instructed him to take deliberate steps through the powder to the tree, and then to turn around and walk back again. He began as she asked, almost stamping in the effort to leave clear footprints, and then wobbling as he almost lost his balance with the exaggerated stepping. He carefully walked the powdered route to the tree and back again to where Alyssa waited with the remains of the carrots.

He needed to take a giant step to move out of the spray of icing sugar. Alyssa extended her hand to him as he stared at the ground uncertainly.

"Over here… step towards me."

He grasped her hand and as he took a large step in her direction, she moved backwards allowing enough space for him to land well clear of the powder. She giggled softly as he lurched off-balance, leaning against her. Letting go of her hand, he grasped her by the shoulders.

"I wasn't expecting Santa's little helper to turn up, but I'm glad you did."

"Really?"

"Really." He pulled her close with a wicked gleam in his eye. "I should consider an appropriate reward."

He kissed her. Not a nice merry Christmas kiss, but a challenging and passionate kiss that asked for and promised more. When they broke apart, Alyssa found herself gasping for breath. It could almost have been corny, but a sudden weakness in her knees resulted in her clinging to him.

"Wow! Where did that come from?"

"You don't object? Perhaps we had some unfinished business. It seemed to me you might even have enjoyed it."

"I might have… just a bit. Are you going to do that again? If you are, perhaps we should take it inside rather than on your front doorstep. I have visions of Emma turning up at any minute."

Just mention of the other woman was enough to galvanise him into action. He pulled her through the doorway and back into the house. They made it as far as the hallway before he pushed her up against the wall and kissed her again. He braced himself against the wall with one hand and trailed a tantalizing path down her body with the other.

Her response was immediate. This hadn't been her intention when she arrived at his door, but now that he'd pressed that sensory button, she didn't want him to stop. A faint sound came from Jeremy's room. They froze, straining to hear against their thumping hearts. There was another murmur and then all was quiet again.

"He often mumbles in his sleep," Max said. "He'll have dropped off again."

"I should be going," Alyssa said reluctantly. "What if he wakes up and finds us like this?"

"What if he does? I can't think of any good reason for you to leave right now. If we adjourn to somewhere quieter, we won't be making out in the passage."

She pulled back to look at him. "Making out… is that what we're doing?"

He pursed his lips as though considering an important question. "I'm out of practice, but I think that's what you call it. C'mon."

He seized her by the hand and led her further down the passage to a room she hadn't been in before. "I might be rusty, but I'm reliably told it's like riding a bicycle. You never forget how."

"Forget how to…?"

He shut the door of what was obviously his bedroom. "How to make love to a challenging and argumentative woman, particularly one who comes bearing gifts of carrots."

She stifled a giggle. "I could have thought that through a bit more. It was an impromptu decision."

"I'm glad about that. Shut up and kiss me again."

They stumbled towards the bed and then fell onto it. In spite of the tangle of limbs, Alyssa managed to undo the buttons of his shirt and ran her hands over his chest, exploring the taunt skin and muscle beneath. He eased her onto her back, and as he did, caressed her breast and eased one leg between hers, exerting gentle pressure against an area that called out for it, all the while managing to deliver nibbling kisses down the side of her neck and into the hollow of her shoulder. The flickering sensation of lips and tongue left her squirming with a mixture of delight and anticipation.

With one hand resting comfortably on her belly, he pulled back so that he could look her in the eyes. "This might not be how you planned on spending your Christmas Eve. It hadn't crossed my mind either, but I'd be lying if I hadn't wanted to take things further on a couple of occasions. If you tell me to stop, I will."

"She reached up and wrapped an arm around the back of his neck, drawing his head close again. "Do you think I would have let things progress this far if I didn't want it? Shut up and kiss me again."

As he eased the skirt of her dress up and over her thighs with his fingers beginning an upward exploration, Alyssa wrapped her legs around him. It was close but not enough. She sat up quicky, pulling her dress up and over her head, sitting there in lacy bra and panties and feeling totally shameless. She took his hand and placed it over her breast. He eased the covering lace to one side and swirled the pebbled peak with his tongue. She gave small mewls in response to the exquisite torture.

"Take it off," she whispered, pushing at the shoulders of his shirt. She needed to feel his skin against hers. As he shrugged the shirt off, she deftly unclipped the catch of her bra and flung it to one side. He kissed one rosy peak and then the other, before beginning a teasing, exploratory journey down the rest of her body, moaning his own satisfaction as she opened up to him.

Their love-making resulted in an urgent coupling, expressing a hunger that each of them had denied up until that point. Once sated, they lay entwined, exhausted but still wanting the physical contact.

"I could easily drift off to sleep here," Alyssa murmured as her fingers traced a lazy path through the golden hairs on his chest. "I'm feeling incredibly relaxed right now."

"Why don't you?"

"Jeremy, that's why. He'll be awake early. Wanting to see me tomorrow is one thing, but finding me in your bed is another. I'll be back early, I promise."

"You're probably right. I was letting my dick rule my head. I'll try not to do it again."

As long as it's with me. She kissed him lightly in response, and slid off the bed and quickly dressed.

"I'll walk out to the car with you." He pulled on his jeans and they tiptoed up the passage, then circumnavigated the snowy footprints they'd created earlier.

Alyssa turned to face him at the car. "I'll be back late morning. If you change your mind, give me a call and let me know."

Max placed a finger across her lips and shook his head. "For an intelligent woman, you talk too much rubbish. He kissed her again.

She kept her promise. Tiger received some unexpected fishy treats for breakfast, after which she unpacked her bags and notified her neighbour of the change in plans. She couldn't turn up empty-handed, so resorted again to a tub of ice cream, purchased at exorbitant expense from the local convenience store, which stocked basic grocery items. Prices were double those found in a normal supermarket, but that was the price of convenience.

Jeremy heard her arrive and tore out of the house, full of excitement. "I thought you weren't coming. Do you know what Santa brought me?" He bombarded her with chatter about Santa's visit, the reindeer and of course, his presents. He accepted the change of plans without further question.

Max followed at a more leisurely pace, with a dopey grin on his face. He leaned forward to kiss her. "Merry Christmas."

"Dad, you kissed Alyssa."

"Yeah, I did, mate. Is that okay?"

"Sure. Thank you for my Lego kit Alyssa. Can you help me put it together?"

"I thought you wanted me to help you," Max protested.

"You can," his son admitted kindly, "but Alyssa knows all about Lego."

"If that's the case, I suppose I can make some Christmas drinks. I assume I'm capable of that."

"Yes, that would be good, Dad."

Max's eyebrows hit the roof, and he exchanged a bemused look with Alyssa before busying himself with the approved task. He made a lemonade spider for Jeremy, using the ice cream that Alyssa had brought, and champagne and orange juice for himself and Alyssa. They toasted each other's health, solemnly clinking glasses.

"It's good that Alyssa came, isn't it Dad?"

"Absolutely. She might spend some more time with us, if we ask her nicely."

"Okay." Jeremy focused on looking for the right piece of Lego.

Max raised his glass again to Alyssa. "Looks like you have the seal of approval."

With Jeremy still sorting his Lego pieces, they wandered onto the patio, overlooking the Bay. The sky was mostly clear blue, with light, white candy fluff on the horizon. In the distance, she could just make out family groups setting up for their picnic lunch on the beach, and a couple of paragliders soared above the bay, weaving with the air currents in a form of aerial dance. Boats headed out from the local ramp, perhaps hoping to catch a snapper for Christmas lunch. Either that, or they wanted to escape the festive chaos at home.

Two children tore up and down the street on their bikes, probably recently delivered by Santa. Their excited shrieks broke the silence. Something smelled good. Alyssa couldn't see it but knew what it would be. One of their neighbours had fired up the grill to make an early start on the barbecue, and already the tantalizing smell of roasting meat wafted in their direction.

Max draped an arm over her shoulder, giving her a light squeeze. "It's a beautiful day out there today. I can't imagine why one would live anywhere else."

Alyssa sipped her drink, relishing the sweet effervescent explosion. She smiled in response, but there was no need to comment. In returning to Sandy Bay, she'd come home in more ways than one.

The End

If you enjoyed this book, please leave a review where you purchased it, or on Goodreads or Bookbub.
Scan the QR Code to find the various links or type linktr.ee/emilyhusseyauthor into your browser

Your comments will help me to provide great stories and will interest future readers.

Don't miss out on your free download!

If you enjoyed this story, you might like to read a collection of short stories in

Romance in the Stone

To receive your *free* copy, and keep up-to-date with news about future releases,

copy and paste https://bit.ly/3qQdbqR into your browser.

Sandy Bay Series

THE AUSTRALIAN COASTAL town of Sandy Bay is close enough to the Adelaide that its residents can access the city if they need to, but far enough away that they can ignore the city too. The town swells with visitors on weekends or during the holiday season, but at other times it's quiet and the locals like it like that.

In a small-town environment, everyone knows everyone else, and secrets can be difficult to keep. It's astonishing what things some people manage to hide for so long. Either in Sandy Bay, or the adjoining hub of Port Reilly, the unexpected may still surprise the most cynical resident.

No matter what the current crisis, the lure of the Bay and the pristine Australian beaches will continue to delight, not just the characters but the readers as well.

The Letters – a short story

JACINTA HAD LOVED spending holidays with her aunt in Pt Reilly. Her aunt was an artist, and they often spent time wandering up and down the coastal area, while Cynthia worked on her latest seascape and Jacinta swam or collected shells.

On arrival at the seaside cottage each year, she would check that nothing had changed. She found reassurance in the consistency of the things in the house, the times they shared together, and her aunt's unquestioned presence.

Except one day Cynthia wasn't there anymore, and Jacinta learned that the house, its contents, and its memories had been left to her. As she sorted through the last of her aunt's worldly possessions, she discovered the tragedy that had shaped the path of Cynthia's life.

Secrets in Sandy Bay – an introductory novella

IT WAS LATE on a Friday afternoon, but was that any excuse?

Property Manager Maddie's heart sinks when she realises that she has given Alex Isherwood the wrong keys to his rental cottage. It's already dark and the weather is foul and promising to get worse. There's no other option – she has to drive out to Seaspray Cottage and sort out this mess.

Give him the keys – that was all she had to do. So how was it that an hour later, she was sitting in front of an open fire, minus her own clothes, and sharing a meal with a man who didn't take 'No' for an answer? The tempest outside was nothing to the storm that was stirred up inside the cottage.

With a shared history in the town, they had a few things in common, but didn't know how much. It's amazing how tightly held some secrets can be, even in a small town where everyone knows everything.

Maddie's world disintegrates as the secrets of her past are revealed.

Escape to Sandy Bay

ALYSSA NEEDS TO escape… from her job, her dreams, and her man. She flees to coastal Sandy Bay to lick her wounds. The town of her childhood holidays provides a job and a place to stay.

Her new-found sanctuary is shattered when she learns of a controversial proposal that will change the face of the sea front forever. When she sees a man undertaking preliminary site investigations, Alyssa springs into action, determined to thwart the development.

Max is focused on caring for his young son and building the reputation of his business. He's not looking for trouble, but in the guise of a lawyer who is quick to react, trouble comes looking for him. She stirs the emotions in ways he didn't expect, but when she neglects his son, he is quick to lash out.

Leaving the past behind is not so easy, especially with unfinished business back in the city. Should she forgive and forget, or forge a new life so different to the one she'd always imagined? The responses of the men in her life influence the decision she needs to make, but which choice is the right one?

Return to Sandy Bay

DELIA FLED SANDY BAY with a secret she couldn't share. She left behind the carefree life that young people enjoyed in the coastal town. She also left behind the man she loved, resolutely forging a future and career in the city.

Work draws her back to the town in which she grew up, forcing her to confront her past and the people who shaped it. Some facts are easily manipulated, and not all actions are honourable. She can't hide the truth from Ben any longer, but there are surprises in store for both of them.

As one door in her life closes, another opens in the form of a new business opportunity, potentially bringing them closer together. She hadn't counted on the changing family dynamics when she made this move.

Will she give Ben a second chance, or will the fallout tear them apart?

Emily Hussey

EMILY HUSSEY HAS lived in several Australian states, and that experience has provided useful backdrop for some of her novels. She spent her twenties in Alice Springs, which became the setting for the Red Centre Series. She now resides on the coast in the city of Adelaide, and is exploring the writing options in every café in walking distance.

Emily was a marriage celebrant for 24 years, and has married couples in many different locations, ranging from private gardens, to beaches, to caves, or rural locations. Many of her clients remain friends to this day. She usually writes with Iris, a black and white cat at her elbow, demanding her share of attention. Writing tends to be fuelled with regular coffee boosts, and occasional squares of very dark chocolate.

9 780648 297246